ARKANSAS HEAT

A

CITY SCORNED

Volume One

BY

KAREN MARIE COLEMAN

Karen Coleman

ISBN: 978-1-7328314-5-2

Kaidonya Brunson
PUBLISHING

Visit our official website at:

www.karencoleman.org

Table of Contents

PROLOGUE

Early Dawn

With the knowledge of a sadistic killer on the loose, the city is gripped with fear, and citizens are on high alert as the bodies of young women are turning up all over town. As imminent danger looms, authorities are warning local women to be mindful of their surroundings.

An employee of the Wiley towing service was getting an early start to his day. After gathering his tools and safety gear, he placed them on his work truck and hopped inside. He grabbed his mic and cued it to inform the morning dispatcher that he was on duty.

"Truck two-thirteen to dispatch."

"Go ahead, truck two-thirteen," answered the husky female voice on the other end of the CB radio.

"Dispatch; truck two-thirteen is on duty; the time is five o'clock a.m."

"That's a big ten-four."

The driver hung his mic on the lever and lowered the CB volume. He turned on his police scanner and exited the dirt-filled driveway into the haunting darkness of the densely wooded area. As he continued onward towards town, he noticed in the near distance what appeared to be a stalled vehicle with the headlights off. With a click of his high beams, it revealed a metallic BMW sedan sitting roadside with hazard lights blinking. Supposing someone was having car trouble due to the car's awkward location, the tow truck driver pulled alongside the vehicle. After retrieving his flashlight and exiting his truck, he approached the vehicle for a closer look. Movement from inside caught his eye. His vision was limited due to condensation on the windows and the early morning dew that had settled on the vehicle's outer surface. He popped his flashlight on, and in a sweeping motion, he aimed it toward the car's back window. The occupant appeared to be asleep. He knocked on the window and tried opening the door, but it was locked. He shined his light inside and continued knocking on the window, trying to get the person's attention.

Blinded by the bright beams from the flashlight, the man inside covered his eyes with his hand. He heard the banging on the window. Checking his surroundings, he noticed he was lying in the back seat of his vehicle with his underwear and cargo shorts around his ankles. He looked down at his limp penis and saw that he was wearing a condom. Lying on the floor next to him was the body of a woman of African American descent. He tried recalling the events that led to his current predicament. He gave an empty gaze to the tow truck driver. Feeling lethargic, and drowsy, he was too weak to move. He lay back in his seat. His eyes rolled in the back of his head, and he blacked out. The banging on the window continued with the voice of the tow truck driver outside yelling,

"Hey Buddy, are you okay in there?" The large white man guided the light, peering in the window, trying to see if his assistance was needed. He walked around to the other side of the vehicle for a closer look. His heart stopped immediately. He was horrified when he saw the partially nude, limp body of a woman on the floor with a rope around her neck. He frantically backed away from the vehicle and ran to his truck as if his life depended on it. He called his dispatcher who in turn notified the police. He remained on the scene but backed his vehicle a safe distance away.

Police arrived a few minutes later. Three officers strategically parked their squad cars, blocking off any potential traffic coming through the area.

By now, the sun was over the horizon, and the scene was more visible. Two officers approached the vehicle with caution. They didn't know if they had two victims or if one was a killer and the other a victim. Once they felt secure, the female officer notified her superior of what they'd found. She requested an ambulance for the unconscious man. It was too late for the female. They could clearly see she was already deceased. While waiting for the paramedics and investigators, crime scene tape was affixed to the police cars, cordoning off the area.

The man in the car was awakened by the female police officer who was trying to take his pulse. With a latex-gloved hand, she carefully reached inside the vehicle, only touching his wrist where necessary so as not to disturb any evidence. She noticed the expensive designer Cartier watch on his wrist, a watch that was given to him by a very close friend. It was a gift of appreciation for him having saved her life. She quickly scanned the car: an unlikely crime scene, a very handsome, well-groomed black man lying in the back seat of an immaculately clean late-model BMW. The scene seemed a bit off to her. There were no signs of a struggle in the car, and everything seemed to be in place except for the obvious. The deceased woman was lying on her back, sprawled across the floor, looking as if she had been stuffed in the car at the last minute. Her left knee was to her chest; her other leg had fallen in the open position, exposing her cleanly shaved genitals. Her head dangled backward on the floorboard with the rope still around her neck. Ligature marks were visible. She was wearing a yellow blouse with large floral prints that was lifted to her braless breasts, and she was wearing a small navel ring. Her underwear was not found inside the vehicle. The officer observed the plaid short-sleeved shirt that the man was wearing was stained with vomit, and his body was drenched in sweat. He appeared to be intoxicated. Incoherent, he had to be physically removed from the vehicle and was placed in the waiting ambulance. Once it was determined that he would be okay, his clothing was removed, as well as his underwear and the condom he was wearing, and placed into evidence bags. A sheet was loosely placed over his body. His watch and necklace had been removed, and his dark brown leather shoes were placed in evidence bags. Hand preservation bags were placed over both his hands to preserve trace evidence until the forensic team could examine them. The man appeared to be in and out of consciousness. Authorities allowed him to rest until they could question him. The police began to assess the area, and a team of detectives began the task of working on the case.

The scene was all too familiar to homicide detective Byron Armstrong, with the exception of finding anyone with a body. It appears as if the authorities may have caught their killer red-handed. This was the sixth consecutive homicide of a female killed in what police are calling the *Scorned* killings, namely because after each killing, an envelope with a card inside is sent to the media and city hall with the location of a body, a head count of the killings and one simple word, *"Scorned."*

The killer's latest victim is Charlene Jackson. She was a local sex worker with a criminal history of soliciting prostitution, drug use, paraphernalia, and other petty crimes. Detective Armstrong was alarmed when he recognized the man found in the back seat of the car with the body. He was a former colleague and a close friend named Blaine Cooper. Seeing his friend in this predicament, he felt sorry for him, but more than that, he knew he needed to explain the events that had taken place. The logical thing for the anxious detective to do was to try and set aside his personal feelings while thoroughly investigating the crime, allowing the evidence to speak for itself. While carefully surveying the scene, he tried to wrap his mind around what he was witnessing. He was hoping to explain away anything that would point to his friend's guilt, but no matter how hard he tried, all evidence collected appeared to implicate him. He continued assessing the scene.

The ambulance doors opened, and the female officer began questioning the male subject.

"Sir, what's your name?"

"Blaine Cooper," he replied in a whispery voice.

"Do you know the young lady in the vehicle?"

Confused and pleading with her through eye contact to help him remember what happened the previous night, he expected her to fill in the blanks for him. He asked,

"Ma'am, where am I?"

She responded with a question of her own.

"Sir, do you know the young lady in the vehicle?"

"No, I don't; what's going on ma'am?"

"That's what I'm waiting for you to tell me," she said.

"Ma'am, I don't know what's going on." He tried to lift himself from the gurney. He looked to his right and noticed his hand was cuffed to the side of the rail. He noticed the evidence bags on his hands, which caused further panic. "What's going on? Let me go!"

She placed her hand on his knee and said, "Calm down Mr. Cooper." He became upset and again demanded to be released. He refused to answer any more questions and was taken to the hospital with a police escort and an officer inside the ambulance. After he was examined, a toxicology screen, hair samples, and other DNA evidence were collected, and he was taken to the county jail and booked for the crime of murder in the first degree.

CHAPTER ONE

Jessica exhaled as she entered the entry door to her home. She threw her keys on the coffee table, went into the kitchen, and fixed herself a glass of vodka. Her feet were sore after being on a two-day stake-out that consisted of jumping fences, being chased by a large pit bull, and standing for long periods. She bore tiny abrasions and mosquito bites from hanging in the brush while trying to stay close to her target. She was also drained because of the unbearable Arkansas heat. She reached for the elastic band that was holding her ponytail up and kicked her sneakers from her feet. She still had clients to see later in the day, so she only had a few hours to rest. Her schedule was hectic, and she was at it non-stop. Regardless of the dangers and uncertainty of the job, she was addicted to the action and wouldn't trade it for anything. Against her father's wishes, Jessica chose a career in law enforcement after college. She planned to work for a couple of years with the police department and then move on to the FBI.

Her father, Jack Barnes, a prominent business owner, was upset that she would consider going into a field so dangerous. After several unsuccessful attempts to get her to reconsider, he finally gave her his blessing. She left the police force and opened her own agency, where she still works to this day.

Jessica removed her shirt and bra, took a few sips of vodka, and fell face down on the bed. In an instant, she was asleep.

The shrill, high-pitched sound of her ringing cell phone broke the silence in the room, waking her. While reaching for the phone, she knocked over the unfinished glass of vodka. "Shit!" Her disheveled hair hung down her back with strands tousled about her deep, warm brown face. She answered without opening her eyes. It was her friend Marcus Miller.

"Good morning baby!" Marcus' voice sounded as though he were speaking through a bullhorn. Pain shot through her head like fireworks going off on Independence Day. She could feel her head throbbing with each pump of blood that flowed through. She removed the phone from her ear. She was a bit annoyed because she longed for the moment when she could lie in her bed and sleep.

"Hi Marcus, what's up?" she asked while exhaling.

"I'm checking on you this morning before I leave. I'm headed to Dallas on business."

"Marcus, you know you don't have to let me know your every move. It's not that serious," she said while still lying in her same sleeping position.

"I know, but I just wanted you to know anyway. I'll be back in a few days; perhaps I can see you when I return?" He was posing the question to her in the hopes she would say yes.

"We'll see. Have a safe trip, okay," she said, trying to sound a bit more sincere. She figured she owed him that much for the many nights of intimate pleasure they shared. She knew she would need him soon, but for now, she needed rest. After ending the call, she looked at the clock and noticed it was nine-thirty.

She tried going back to sleep, but the sun was shining directly into her bedroom windows. Normally, she would enjoy the sunshine. What she'd once considered a nice feature of floor-to-ceiling windows when she bought the house, she found a bit annoying when she was trying to sleep. She went into her back bedroom to get more sleep. As soon as she dozed off, her phone rang. This time it was her home phone. She decided to let it ring. She breathed a sigh of relief when it stopped. It began ringing once more. Now irritated, she answered it only to get rid of the caller. She was familiar with the male voice on the other end. It was her good friend Blaine Cooper, the very guy who was found unconscious with the dead female. Blaine was a former police officer who moonlighted as a part-time detective at her agency. In addition to assisting with investigations, he's used as a backup guy when she needs a little muscle on the street. He sounded distraught but was relieved that she'd answered his call.

"Jessica! Thank God you finally picked up."

"Blaine?"

"Yeah, it's me, Jessie. Listen to me because I don't have long to talk. I'm in the county jail, and I need your help."

"What's going on Blaine? What are you doing in jail?"

"I've been arrested and charged with murder."

"Murder?" she said in disbelief. She wasn't sure if she was hearing him correctly.

"Blaine, are you kidding? What happened?"

"I don't know," he said. He was taking deep breaths, trying to calm himself, but it wasn't working.

"I can't go into great detail right now, but I can tell you that they think I'm responsible for the string of *Scorned* murders."

"What! You've got to be kidding me."

"No, I'm not. Can you please do me a favor?"

"Yes Blaine, whatever it is, you know I'll do it."

"I need you to stop by my place and get some clothes for my court hearing. They took my clothes, shoes, and even my underwear for evidence. If you don't bring me something to wear, I'll have to go to my hearing in jail clothes. The hearing is at eleven-thirty. The only person they'll allow to visit me at this time is my attorney, but you can get the clothes to her, and she can bring them to me. How soon can you do that?" he asked nervously.

"I don't think they'll allow you to change clothes, but I'll stop by your place anyway. Let me get dressed. I'll be on my way. Where's your attorney?"

"She's on her way, but I want you there too.

"I'll be there."

17

Jessica scrambled for her robe and called the police station. Although she was no longer employed with L.R.P.D., she had many connections on the force and often worked parallel investigations with a few of her favorite detectives. She spoke with one of the detectives who briefed her on why Blaine was arrested and told her everything he could legally share with her. Realizing Blaine was telling the truth, she was stunned at the news. She ended the call and took a shower.

The sudden blast of tepid water on her face sobered and refreshed her. As she was showering, she began thinking about Blaine, *"This must be a mistake. The police have the wrong guy."* She knew her friend, and she knew he wasn't a killer, and any evidence they had on him had to be circumstantial. But being caught in the backseat of a car with a dead woman is pretty damning evidence, she thought as she continued her shower.

Blaine worked in law enforcement for sixteen years. He's an ex-military war vet, having served several tours of active duty.

Once, while Blaine and Jessica were out on a domestic violence call, a violent suspect who'd stabbed his girlfriend tried to kill Jessica when she intervened to help the dying woman. He grabbed her from behind, placed the knife to her throat, and pressed it into her skin. Blaine was able to subdue him, causing him to release his hold on Jessica. Jessica still has the scar. Although they were partners, they formed a close bond that sealed their friendship. She'll do anything for him and feels indebted to him for saving her life. She tried repaying him, but he wouldn't hear of it. Blaine had his eye on a particular Cartier watch. He had been talking about it for a few months, but with a wife, a mortgage, and two young kids, he couldn't see purchasing such a lavish gift for himself. Armed with that information, Jessica purchased the watch and insisted on him taking it, but he refused. After much pressure from her and her father, he finally accepted.

He's a man of good moral character and principles. Although divorced, he and his ex-wife remain close, choosing to co-parent their two young sons. He's the head coach for his son's little league baseball team, the guy who's loved by everyone, who can do no wrong, and who has no enemies. He'll go out of his way to help anyone, especially those less fortunate. Blaine is the owner of a fitness gym in the central Little Rock area. He teaches martial arts and self-defense classes for women and children. He's well-loved in his community, so for him to be accused of murder was shocking.

Jessica got dressed and drove towards Blaine's place. She called her office to fill her mother in on the information Blaine had given her. Her mother, Annette Barnes, worked for her at the detective agency. She's a feisty retired paralegal. Although she's in her early sixties, she can easily pass for forty-five years or younger. She's highly energetic and can put most people half her age under the table with her strict workout regimen. She's also a part-time fitness instructor in Blaine's gym. She loves going undercover for Jessica when needed and is always up for a challenge. She enjoys working with her daughter. She says, *"Somebody's got to keep her in line."* Annette picked up the ringing phone.

"Barnes Detective Agency."

"Hi Mom," Jessica said.

"Good morning, darling. How are you this morning?"

"Mom, I really can't talk right now. I called to tell you that Blaine's in trouble and he needs me. He's been arrested."

"Our Blaine was arrested? What for?"

"He told me he was arrested for murder."

"Girl, hush your mouth!" her mother said.

"Mom, I need you to cancel my two-thirty appointment. See if they'll reschedule for a later date. I'm heading to Blaine's place to get him something to wear for his court hearing. I'll call you later."

"Keep me posted baby. Call me if you need me."

"Okay, mom. I have to go."

Jessica made it to Blaine's home. He lived in the Otter Creek part of town located in southwest Little Rock. She almost didn't recognize the neighborhood when she pulled onto Blaine's street, a place she'd traveled to every week. She noticed the area was swarming with investigators, media, and curious onlookers. The media had the neighborhood streets littered with cords from their camera equipment and blocking traffic. There were many large vans with satellite dishes perched high as most reporters focused on the small two-story structure in a normally peaceful neighborhood. The neighbors were annoyed by all the unwanted attention, most fearing their property values would decrease by having a suspected serial killer in their neighborhood. They were equally alarmed because most of them knew Blaine. He had been a guest in their homes as well as a host of many neighborhood parties at his own home; some felt as though they dodged the bullet when word of his arrest was made public. His neighbors hadn't noticed any signs of him being a killer. Jessica finally made it through but had to park a few houses down the street and walk the rest of the way to the home. She looked around for the official in charge. That person was her former Lieutenant Gary Fitz.

"Lieutenant," she spoke as she walked up to him. He was a tall, thin, white gentleman in his late fifties who always complained about his knees but had never done anything about them.

"Hi there, Private Investigator Jessica Barnes," he said trying to keep a straight face without laughing at her.

"How's that working out for you? You know that private thing that you do?" He was taking a pun at her career move. He felt that she belonged on the force and never should've resigned. She wasn't interested in his opinions on her career choice. Feeling a bit annoyed by his poor attempt to tease her, she produced an evil glare, then rolled her eyes and snarled,

"You may want to come and work for me. I can always use an extra guy on my team. I have a highly successful business, and things couldn't be better. The last time I checked, I found that I was still rich. It seems like you can read a chapter from my book, but what about you? How are those knees of yours? Have you been staying off of them lately, or are you still kneeling and kissing ass at the department? That reminds me; I need to add knee pads and lip balm to my Christmas list. I'm sure you can make use of them."

His cheeks turned a bright shade of pinkish red, and the smile on his face turned into a curious frown. He reached for his handkerchief and wiped the sweat from his brow. After stuffing it back into his pocket, he moved towards Jessica and said,

"Still quite the smart ass, huh? Always hitting below the belt. Get your smart ass over here and give me a hug, damn it." She smiled, and they hugged briefly.

"You know I love you, Lieutenant. How's Helen doing?" she asked, speaking of his wife.

"Oh, she's doing great, still complaining that I'm not spending enough time with her. She keeps hounding me to have the knee surgery and perhaps go into early retirement, but I can't do that right now. I had to go and get her a pooch to hold her off for a while. We'll see how long that'll last."

"So, how long are you guys going to be here?"

"As long as it takes," said Lieutenant Fitz.

"Well, I need to get a suit for him to go to court this morning. How possible is that?"

He shook his head and said, "Sorry, it's not happening. They aren't letting anybody in at this time. You know the drill."

"Yeah, I know. Have they found anything yet?"

"Nothing useful. They're still gathering evidence, though." She looked on as the detectives brought bags and boxes from Blaine's place that they felt could be pertinent to their case.

"Is Armstrong in there?"

"Yeah, he's in there, but you may not want to bother him. He's been as mean as a snake ever since he had to charge Blaine. Captain's been breathing down his neck about the case all morning. He didn't want to take it. He asked to be reassigned, but his request was denied. Now he's taking it out on everybody. Captain felt he was the best man for the job, and perhaps he'd be eager to solve the crime because of their friendship. Since Blaine *is* a former officer from this department, they want to get this crime solved. Still, Armstrong isn't comfortable with the case, but it's not always about what's comfortable but what's right. It's always difficult when you have to arrest one of your own, especially a good friend like Blaine.

"I understand," she said. "I won't bother him now. I'll get with him another time. I have to get going; I need to get Blaine something to wear to court."

Lieutenant Fitz looked up at Jessica with concern and asked,

"How's he doing?"

"I don't know. I haven't gone to see him yet. I spoke with him by phone, but he didn't sound well."

"When you see him, you tell him to hang in there."

"Do you think that he's guilty of these crimes?" she asked out of curiosity. Sucking his teeth and shaking his head, he said,

"Knowing Blaine as I do, I would say no, but they caught him with the body. I dunno anymore. I mean, how well do you really know people nowadays? Just when you think you know somebody, they go and get themselves caught with a dead body. I can't speak for or against him. But it doesn't sound like the Blaine I know."

"Well, I'm sure he'll appreciate your confidence in him," she said with a hint of sarcasm. "Oh, and lieutenant…"

"Yeah, Barnes."

"You really ought to consider having the surgery." She walked away.

She purchased a suit and a pair of shoes for Blaine, hoping she'd chosen the right size, and drove to the county jail. Rushing down Roosevelt Road, she hoped she would be there in time for him to change, but when she got there, he had already been transported to the county courthouse. She returned the clothes to her car and drove to the courthouse downtown. It was only about a fifteen-minute drive from the jail. She found it difficult to find a parking spot when she made it. After circling the block of the historical building and having no success, she parked in the parking garage of a nearby hotel. She walked across the street and went inside, taking the elevator to the second floor. As she stepped off the elevator, she saw the news media camped out. The courtroom was filled to capacity, and people were spilling out into the hallway. She was forced to remain in the hall. When the court proceedings were over, the crowd began to shuffle around as Blaine was escorted out by four deputy sheriffs, one in front, two at his side, and one in the rear. Microphones and audio recorders were being shoved in Blaine's face as the many news reporters tried to interview him as he walked down the hallway. A slender black female reporter said,

"Mr. Cooper you were found with the sixth body. Are you the Scorned killer?" His attorney, Karen Reed, a well-known African American defense attorney in the state, stepped in and answered most of the questions.

"My client has no comment at this time."

"The police say that your client was caught basically red-handed. With him being an ex-cop, he could've easily committed these killings, especially since he knows police procedures; what do you have to say about that?" Again, stepping forward in the defense of her client, his attorney said,

"When the evidence is presented, my client will be exonerated and cleared of all the charges against him." The lovely, tall, mocha-toned woman looked confident, poised, and distinguished in her designer suit with matching accessories. Her long dark brown hair with cinnamon highlights was curled to perfection. Her make-up was flawless. She gently but effectively pushed through the reporters with her briefcase in hand. She got in the elevator with her client and the deputies and went to the first floor, then out the back door. Jessica, who had been forced to take another elevator caught up to them. Blaine was being placed in the transport van to be sent back to the county jail. Before he got inside, Jessica yelled out to him,

"I'll be down there." He nodded his head and got in the van.

At the jail, Jessica was allowed to visit Blaine. It was strange seeing her friend in the orange jumpsuit. She looked at him with sympathy. She saw the pain and fear on his face. She wanted so badly to hold him and tell him everything was going to be okay. Her heart ached to see him so distraught, but she knew she had to pull herself together. She studied his face closely. His eyes were bloodshot red, and his dark brown skin, which once glowed, appeared dull and dry. The large jumpsuit hid his athletic build.

"How are you holding up?" she asked as she took a seat. She knew the answer to the question, but she tried to open with a little small talk. A thick glass partition separated them, with a speaker in it. He had a somber expression on his face.

"I'm not doing too well," he said.

"I'm confused, and I don't know what's happening. This whole thing is crazy." He looked up at her after holding his head down for a moment.

"Please promise me that you'll check on my boys. See to it that they're protected until this is over. Let'em know I love them," he said, looking as if he was trying to hold back his emotions.

"I will," she said, looking at him sympathetically. "I know that Shelia and her fiancé will do everything to protect them as well."

"Yeah, I'm glad she has Virgil. He's a good man."

"Have you talked with her yet?" Jessica asked.

"No, not yet.

"Well, I'll stop by there," she said, reassuring him.

"So, can you tell me what happened?" Jessica asked.

"I can tell you what I can remember," he said, eager to tell his side of the events. "After my self-defense class, I drove to the pub downtown and grabbed a few drinks with some of the guys. After a couple of beers and a few games of pool, I began feeling very ill. I couldn't drive, so I had the bartender call me a taxicab. When I walked outdoors, one was already waiting, so I went inside. I don't remember anything after that. The next thing I knew, I was awakened by a police officer. I was lying in the back seat of my car with my pants down to my ankles. I was wearing a condom. The female victim was lying on the floor. She was nude from the waist down. She had been strangled with a rope, and her neck was broken. We were found on the back side of College Station off Thibault Drive."

"Did you know the girl?"

"I've never seen her before and didn't see her at the pub either."

"Okay, so what happened next?"

"After being awakened by the officer, I still felt sick to my stomach. I was vomiting everywhere. I thought it was from drinking, but I don't remember having that much to drink."

Jessica interrupted him; "We'll have to see what the toxicology report says. I'm willing to bet somebody put something in your drink. I'd like to know what happened at that pub. In the meantime, I want you to try and remember everything you can, and we'll start to piece things together. I know you're not guilty. We're going to get to the bottom of this and clear your name. We're going to have to work fast, though. Did you know or recognize anyone at the club? You said you were drinking with a couple of guys and playing pool."

"Yeah, I was with Slim and Cordell."

"Why didn't you get one of them to take you home?"

"They were headed out to the sports bar in West Little Rock, so they left. I just wanted to have a couple of beers, play a little pool, and go home because I had a big day ahead of me. But anyway, I continued to play pool with a couple of other guys."

"Did you know the guys that you were playing pool with?"

"No, I didn't, but I've seen them around the pub a time or two. They were a couple of regulars"

"Who served you drinks at the bar?"

"Two people were working the bar, a male and a lady. He would fix the drinks, and she would bring them to the floor. I think she's kinda new. She looked to be in her mid-twenties. She had black hair and lots of tattoos. It wasn't my first time seeing her, though. I've met her somewhere before but can't quite remember where. Anyway, she was very kind. She brought me both beers."

"Did you visit elsewhere or eat or drink anything before arriving at the pub?"

"No, I only had a sports drink after my class, and I went on down to the pub."

"What does the male bartender look like?"

"You know Jessie, I can't remember. I didn't pay much attention to him. When I saw the guys and we got on the pool table, I was only focused on our pool game.

"Does the pub have cameras?"

"I've never noticed any, but it'll be easy to find out."

"Okay, I'm going to stop by there and take a look around to see what's what. Is there anything else that you can remember about last night?"

"No"

"I'm going to do everything in my power to help clear you. I'll be in touch, okay? Stay strong," she said as she held her fist up to the window, giving him a fist bump. Jessica left the jail and drove downtown to the pub to ask questions.

Everyone there was willing to help, but the information she gained was useless. She also found out that they had no surveillance cameras. She then went down to the police department to speak with a couple of her former colleagues there. After walking through the halls, full of twists and turns that resembled a maze, she stuck her head into each office, speaking as she went. She pushed open a set of doors that led to the office she was looking for. She went over to the desk of a white male with a large muscular build; he was very tall. His massive size intimidated those who were unfamiliar with him. Although he's a hard-nosed detective, he's somewhat of a gentle giant; he was another close friend of Jessica. Byron Armstrong is a homicide detective and twenty-six-year vet of the police department, with nine of those years in the homicide division. He and Jessica worked cases together when she worked in the homicide division. He was on the phone when she walked in. He motioned for her to take a seat. She sat and waited patiently while he continued his phone conversation. She looked at her watch; it was around one-thirty. He had finally ended his call. He stretched a little, exhaled, and said,

"Boy, it's already been a long day."

"Yes, it has. I'm surprised you're here. I thought you would still be at Blaine's place," she said.

"We took everything we needed for today; we couldn't find much…raked over it with a fine-tooth comb. His place was squeaky clean, so I had them shut it down for today. What brings you by? It seems you're here now more than when you were on the force." She flashed a courtesy smile, but he noticed the weary look in her eyes.

"Now Armstrong, don't act like you don't know why I'm here. You know I'm here about Blaine."

"Ah yeah, our good friend Blaine. The look in his eyes when they slammed those bars shut on him was devastating. It hurt me to have to lock him up, but given the circumstances, I had to do my job. I was surprised when I made it to the scene. It's the strangest case I've seen in quite some time. It's already proving to be quite unique. Barnes, there are so many pieces to this puzzle that I don't even know where to begin."

She leaned forward and said, "That's why I want to speak with you. Can you tell me what really happened out there? Blaine was upset and I didn't want to keep pressing him."

As much as Jessica wanted to hear what he had to say, she wanted him to be able to share the information with her freely and without any interruptions, so she asked,

"Have you eaten lunch yet?"

"No, I haven't. You're just in time to take me."

"How about you take me? I picked up the tab last time."

"Oh, you're going to *want* to pay for my meal when I tell you what I know." He grabbed his blazer off the back of his chair, and they left. They took her car and went to a downtown deli that wasn't far from the precinct. Once inside, they proceeded to a small table at the rear of the dining area for a little privacy. When they were seated, Jessica asked,

"So, what do you have to tell me that'll make me want to pay for lunch?" Detective Armstrong looked at her intently and said,

"Barnes, I understand that you and Blaine are close, so I'm going to share a few things with you, but if you say or do anything to undermine this investigation, I swear I'll never share another tip with you again."

"Armstrong, you know me by now. How many times have we shared valuable information with each other? I would never do anything to harm this investigation. All I want is the truth. Now, don't play with me. Spit it out."

"We don't have all the evidence processed on Blaine, but I can tell you that it looks like more than one person is involved."

"What do you mean?"

"The location where we found Blaine's car was processed, and we found drops of oil that had leaked from another vehicle but didn't come from Blaine's car. The drops of oil were behind his car, and skid marks from the tires of that vehicle were leading away from the scene. There was definitely more than one car there. Also, we never found the condom wrapper, although he was wearing a condom. There were no rope burns or fibers on Blaine's hands, although the rope at the scene was the one used to strangle the victim. They're testing it for skin cells and any other DNA they can gather. Perhaps he used gloves, but if so, where are they? There are just too many things about this crime that don't add up. Either Blaine had an accomplice, or he may have been set up. Oh, and here's another thing that bothers me. Now, this clue hasn't been revealed to the public, only to those close to the case. The letters *B.C.* had been carved into the left buttocks of each victim. Since Blaine was found with the body, naturally, we're supposed to believe the initials are his. The strange thing about that is this body had the marks, but there was no knife found at the scene. Did he ditch it along with the gloves? Did he commit the crime someplace else? We have all this information, but nothing's adding up. I don't have all the pieces in place yet, but I'm going to get to the bottom of it."

Jessica sat up in her seat and drew closer to Detective Armstrong. "Blaine said he took a taxi away from the pub, but nobody saw him leave in a taxi. Everybody saw him walk out the door, but he seemingly disappeared. So, if he took a taxi, how did his car end up at the scene and with him in it?"

"He may have decided to drive his car instead of taking a taxi," said Detective Armstrong.

"No, Blaine said there was already a taxi out there when he walked out of the pub. He said he got inside but doesn't remember anything from there. He could've been drugged. When do you expect the toxicology report to be complete?"

"Any evidence involving these killings are given priority, so the full report should take a couple of days, but the unofficial report could be done as early as the morning.

"Well, I'm willing to bet he was drugged before leaving the bar. We all know that Blaine never drinks enough to get drunk. I've never seen him drunk in the years I've known him. He says he only had a couple of beers. So, if we want to explore the possibility of him being drugged, then we must determine if he was drugged at the bar or before he got there. Something must've happened because I know Blaine is innocent. I can't see him harming anyone. It's not in his nature," she said.

"Well, he *was* caught with the body in the back seat of his car with his *pants down*, so to speak, and don't forget, with him being a martial arts instructor and self-defense expert, he could've easily overpowered her. The rope gripped her neck so tightly that it snapped like a pencil. Although a lot of the evidence points directly to him, I still have reservations about this case. Something just doesn't feel right."

"Perhaps the scene was staged to make him appear guilty," she said in the defense of Blaine.

"Look, Barnes, I know you'll do just about anything for him, especially since he saved your life. Hell, he's my friend, too, but we can't deny the obvious. Now, personally, I find it hard to believe that he committed this crime, but I must look at the evidence and not our friendship. I'm going to work on this case from all angles. In the end, the truth will be revealed. Now just between us, I believe there's a possibility that he could've been set up, but we'll have to wait until all the evidence is processed."

She looked at him out of curiosity. "Can you tell me why you believe he may have been set up?"

"Well, along with the carved initials on the body and no knife, the missing condom wrapper, and a few other discrepancies, I was wondering, who goes through all of this to commit a murder and then falls asleep in the process? I mean, Blaine was barely conscious when I saw him. Serial killers are known to be very meticulous. They take pride in their so-called abilities. They enjoy the thrill of the hunt and the kill. The FBI's criminal behavioral analyst assigned to the case predicted a killer with qualities opposite of Blaine. I mean, none of his predictions were accurate. He even had to admit that Blaine didn't fit the description of the killer. Then, after interviewing Blaine and looking at the evidence, I just have a hunch that this is not just an open and shut case; that's all I'm going to say about it."

"Okay then," Jessica said while looking at the menu.

"Order up. I guess I'm paying." They both laugh.

Detective Armstrong's cell phone rang. He answered, and with an exhausting expression on his face, Jessica could tell something was wrong. He gave her a chilling look as he continued to listen to the caller on the other end. He reached into his pocket, got his pen and pad, and scribbled on them. Jessica tried to make out what he'd written, but his handwriting wasn't legible. She waved her hand, motioning for him to tell her what was happening. He finally ended his call and said,

"I've got another body. I have to go."

"What do you mean another body?"

"I'll call you later," he said, rushing out.

"Have you forgotten you're riding with me?"

"Oh shit, that's right. Come take me back to the station."

"How about you let me go with you?"

"I need to go and get my car, but you can follow me, and please don't get in the way." Jessica drove him to the station, and once he got in his vehicle, she followed him.

When they arrived on the scene, Detective Armstrong stepped out of his vehicle. The temperature was a hundred and six degrees and rising. The detective peeled his blazer as he got out of his air-conditioned vehicle. He grabbed his hat to protect his balding head as the sun seemed to angrily focus its attention solely upon him. Jessica climbed out of her vehicle. The wind slightly blew a stench across her nostrils. With the blistering heat and the odor, she thought she would faint. Although she had worked in the homicide division for years, she could never get used to the smell of death. It always seemed to bother her. It wasn't just the smell but the fact that someone died on her watch, and she felt she owed it to the victim and their families to solve the case. She covered her nose and mouth with an extra t-shirt she had lying in her vehicle. She walked over to where Detective Armstrong was standing, and they were ushered to the body by an officer. "She's with me," he said to the officer. He handed her a container of eucalyptus ointment. She opened it, dabbed at it with her finger, and spread it

42

under her nostrils. They walked briskly through the gravel and brush. Lieutenant Fitz was standing near the yellow tape. When he saw Jessica and Detective Armstrong together, he said, "Well, look at you two; it's just like old times. Barnes, this is where you belong, especially since you can't seem to stay away."

"Lieutenant, how many times do we have to have this discussion? I enjoy my freedom and peace of mind. You, of all people, should be able to understand that." She smiled and patted him on the shoulder.

Detective Armstrong lifted the yellow tape for Jessica. After walking a few yards through the weeded area, they finally came upon the body of the white female victim. She was partially nude and had been strangled. Her head was bent so far backward that it appeared as though it was detached from her body. The scene had the tell-tale signs of the *Scorned* killer. She'd been there for a while. The victim was the chief of police's daughter. Her name is Lana Albright. Lana was a twenty-four-year-old college dropout. Her recreational use of drugs and constant partying began to take its toll on her life and schooling, so she moved back in with her parents. Her negative attitude and constant refusal to follow her parents' simple rules prompted them to issue her an ultimatum: either return to college or get a job. After a heated argument with her parents, she left and had been missing for about a week. Her parents thought she was taking some time to cool off, and quite frankly, they needed some time as well, so they never filed a missing person's report.

She was found in a field in the east part of the city, close to the location where Blaine was found with the body of the previous victim, Charlene Jackson. The area was very secluded, just beyond the Pulaski County line, but was within the city's jurisdiction. It was also a place where young couples used to make out and where car thieves dumped stolen cars. The young couple who found her grew up in the area and were familiar with its surroundings. They ditched school to spend time together. While making out, the young man stepped from the vehicle to urinate and stumbled upon her body. He immediately called the authorities.

The unmistakable stench of decaying flesh was ever present as the wind blew. Her body was bloated and filled with gases, and she could burst at any moment. Flies were swarming, and their larvae wriggled on her greying skin. The area was swamped with reporters, and the other officers were trying to keep them at bay. Detective Armstrong was horrified when he recognized the young lady.

"Ahh shit! Are you fucking kidding me?"

"What is it, Armstrong?" Jessica asked.

"Take a closer look at her face. Don't you recognize her?"

"Hard to say she's so swollen. Who is it?"

"It's Lana, the Chief's daughter"

"Are you sure?"

"Yes, I'm sure; he keeps a picture of his family on his desk, and all the years we've worked together, I should know Lana when I see her."

"Oh, this is not good," Jessica said. She knew it was not only bad for the chief but for Blaine as well. She knew they were going to want someone for the crime, and since Blaine was caught with one of the bodies, she was worried they would pin this murder on him, too.

The news reporters asked questions of anyone who answered. One local reporter walked up and placed a microphone in Lieutenant Fitz's face.

"Do you think this murder is connected to the other murders?" He gave her a brief statement.

"We don't know anything definite at this time, and we don't want to speculate. We must continue our investigation before we can issue a statement." The lieutenant tried to leave, but she asked more questions

"Do you think the same guy is responsible for this murder?"

"Again, I won't speculate at this time."

"Can you tell me how long she's been dead?"

"No further comment."

He continued walking as the reporter kept pressing him. After realizing she wasn't going to get any answers from him, she went to Detective Armstrong and asked, "Do you think that Blaine Cooper did this?" Without answering her question, he motioned for an officer.

"Please have the media step back so we can do our job and secure the rest of this area, and don't let anyone cross over here." Detective Armstrong instructed everyone on the scene to remain quiet until next-of-kin could be notified. He didn't mention to anyone else on the scene who the girl was. Only he and Jessica knew for the time being. He was a little upset but didn't allow it to stop him from doing his job. He went over to the body.

"It looks like she's been here for a few days, at least a week or so," he said. He looked at the large ligature mark on her neck and the position of her body. Jessica looked at her. She noticed a few broken nails.

"Looks like she put up a fight," she said. She has broken nails on her right hand and a couple on her left. I hope there are some skin fragments from the killer. It appears she was strangled from behind. They noticed a Durex brand condom wrapper near the body, but no condom was found in the area.

"Where's her underwear?" Jessica asked. Detective Armstrong didn't answer the question. Although she was allowed on the scene she couldn't participate in the investigation. The body was processed and taken away. Jessica stayed on the scene chatting with others as they wrapped up their investigation in the area. She'd worked with most of them. Echoing Lieutenant Fitz, they gave subtle hints expressing that she return to the force. They missed her and enjoyed working with her. She was thoughtful and caring and she was always the life of the party. In addition, she was a damn good detective. Jessica knew leaving was the best move for her, and she assured them that she wasn't interested in returning.

CHAPTER TWO

It was nine-thirty in the morning, and Jessica was getting a late start to her day. She hadn't had much sleep in the past couple of days, and since learning of Blaine's arrest, she'd been running on fumes. By the time her head hit the pillow, she was out like a light.

Her mother's phone call awakened her. She was concerned because she hadn't heard much from Jessica. After chatting with her mother, she showered and fixed breakfast. While eating, she watched the news. The news of Chief Albright's daughter was the lead story. Blaine was being tried in the media. They talked about the case constantly. The story was on just about every local TV station. Local commentators were analyzing and speculating what they thought could've happened. Most of them were trying Blaine in the press. Even the citizens on the streets being interviewed jumped on the bandwagon, expressing their relief at Blaine's arrest, making comments like, *"People can sleep easier now that that animal is off the street."*

Hearing so many people speaking negatively of Blaine bothered Jessica, but she was determined not to lose her focus. She was going to do everything humanly possible to help clear her friend, and she was totally capable, having been on the force as a detective for many years. She solved a significantly high number of homicide cases. While working in the burglary division for a couple of years, she solved a great percentage of the cases that crossed her desk, which was pretty impressive given that burglary crimes were a bit more challenging. Jessica picked up the remote and turned the channel. She was sipping her coffee. She had plans of hitting the streets to conduct her own investigation. She was confident that Blaine was being framed, so she wanted to investigate any enemies of his or anyone holding a grudge from any arrests he may have made when he worked as an officer. She got dressed and drove to Blaine's ex-wife's home to check on his children as he requested. When she arrived, she found Sheila out back working in her garden. The boys were with her.

"Hey Jessie," she said as she looked up from her work. The boys were excited to see her.

"Hi, Auntie Jessica!" They ran into her arms and hugged her.

"Look at what Auntie Jessica brought you." She gave the younger one, Marcell, who was six, a new baseball and Marion, who was eight, a new glove. They were excited, and they quickly ran to the side of the yard to play. She made her way over to Sheila.

"Hey there girl," she said to Jessica while removing her gardening gloves. They made their way to the patio and took a seat.

"It's already hot out here. Can I get you something to drink?"

"No, I'm okay. I have some Gatorade in the car." Jessica looked over at the boys.

"How are they? Do they know?"

"Not yet," Sheila answered, looking heartbroken. Her light grey eyes were worn with concern.

"I haven't had the heart to tell them. I took them out of school to try to protect them, and I've kept the TV turned off so they won't hear the news. Their daddy's images are on every station. I don't want to alarm them. I know this is a horrible mistake, and the police need to hurry and sort it all out. They're making him look as if he were an evil monster in the news. I know Blaine didn't do the things they're accusing him of," she said, looking sad and confused. Her fair skin was moistened with tiny beads of sweat under the warm sun. A few unruly strands of hair stuck to the sides of her face and neck. She pulled at her shirt a few times, fanning it to cool herself, and continued. "Jessica, he's a good man and a wonderful father. How much longer are they going to let this go on, knowing they have an innocent man behind bars?"

Sheila was upset about Blaine's arrest. One would think they were still married the way she was carrying on. They remained close even though they were divorced. Sheila's engaged to Virgil Walker a man she met in Louisiana while visiting her mother. After striking up a conversation, she learned he had family ties in Arkansas. They began to date and two years later were engaged. Regardless of Sheila and Virgil's engagement, things were very cordial between him and Blaine. After twelve years of marriage, Sheila and Blaine decided they were better suited as friends, so they divorced. They chose to co-parent so their children wouldn't suffer from the split. Although their marriage failed, Blaine was happy that she found someone who loved her and their children.

Jessica reassured Sheila that she would help to clear Blaine.

"Trust me, Sheila; we're going to get to the bottom of this. I must admit that the evidence against him is strong, but there's almost too much evidence that makes it a very suspicious case. It smells like a set-up to me. Since he was found in the car, they feel holding him on the charges is necessary. Do you know of any enemies that he may have had, or has he been having problems with anyone lately?"

"Not that I know of, but you know Blaine; if he were having problems, he would keep that to himself. That was one of the issues between us during our marriage. He never seemed to open up to me, especially if he was having problems. I often felt like an outsider. But he's a man's man, and he would die rather than admit to anything bothering him. He seemed to think it made him look weak. But to answer your question, I haven't noticed anything out of the ordinary."

"I'm going to be looking around to see what I can find; in the meantime, you keep your eyes open for anything or anyone suspicious, especially since I believe the real *Scorned* killer is still on the loose. Do you think that you can take the boys and go to your parent's home in Baton Rouge?"

"Actually, Virgil and I planned on going there for a while. I was thinking about telling the boys about their father, but I decided against it, at least for now. I don't want them to lose their innocence or their trust in their dad. I know that if we stay here any longer, they're going to find out eventually. Especially with all the media coverage."

"I understand," she said. "Well, let me know before you leave. It may be a good idea if you go over to the jail to see Blaine. It'll lift his spirits."

"Yes, I'll be going by before we leave for Louisiana," Sheila said.

"Take care," Jessica said. She walked over to hug the boys and left.

She went to Asher Avenue to a popular spot named Cindy's Soirée. It's a five-star restaurant and nightclub that serves great food with wonderful adult entertainment. The shows consisted of a grand, choreographed burlesque style of dance. Also included in the shows was erotic poetry, which was acted out on stage. People from all over were fans of the place. The club is owned by a young lady named Cindy Brooks. She's a tough lady who's had her share of issues. Cindy's biracial. She's a former sex worker and recovering addict. She'd been a confidential informant, and over the years, she'd often given Jessica useful information. Cindy had been one of her many street connections, with her eyes and ears open to the underground world. Anything that went down, Cindy knew about it. Her information was always accurate. In return, Jessica would drop some cash on her.

Cindy has gone legitimate, but she still has connections to the underground dealings of the city. She was a good-hearted person who had suffered from several bad breaks. From an abusive childhood to bad relationships, she'd seen it all, including coping with the untimely death of her only son. After she finally escaped an abusive relationship with a notorious drug lord, she went on the run with her son. She ran to a good friend and mentor named Leslie Spencer. Leslie hid her until she could find a safe place for her and her child. One night, while Cindy was at work, she received a call that the home was on fire and her son Micah and Leslie had died in the fire. The cause of the fire was determined to be accidental.

To cope with the pain, she began drinking and doing drugs while dancing in any strip joint that would hire her. When she got tired of what the drugs were doing to her body, she decided to get clean. She continued to work as a dancer while paying her way through school, earning several degrees. With a great business plan, she secured a bank loan and invested seventy percent of her money into her business. She purchased the club that she now owns.

Jessica turned into the parking lot. Cars were already beginning to pile in. She found an available parking spot and went inside. She noticed Cindy sitting at a table in the front of the club, working on her laptop. Jessica sat with her.

"Erin, bring me a cola over here," Cindy yelled out to the bartender.

"What brings you by, Barnes?"

"I'm sure you've heard the news by now. Blaine's in trouble. I'm here to see if you've heard anything or perhaps know anything that can be of help." Cindy shook her head.

"I haven't heard a thing. When I saw it on the news, it was kinda hard to believe that about Cooper. You two are like peas in a pod. How are you doing?"

"I'm alright, I guess; I'm more concerned about Blaine."

"I have to tell ya, Barnes, I don't believe what they're saying about him. He's a good man. He's always treated me and the girls well. There were many times that he should've taken us to jail, but instead, he would pull us aside and talk to us, giving us words of wisdom instead of hauling us in. There were plenty of nights that Cooper took me home to keep me out of trouble. If he wanted to hurt any of us, he would've done it long before now. He never once asked for any sexual favors, and trust me, a few of them do. He was kind to us, even buying food when he knew that we hadn't eaten anything. When I saw the story on the news this morning, I knew they had the wrong guy. They say they caught him with Charlene's body. I knew Charlene well. I tried to reach out and help her, but she wasn't ready. I was confused when Cooper was arrested. I can remember thinking that if they caught him with the body, then he must be guilty. I tried to wrap my mind around it. I just decided to wait to see how it plays out."

Jessica showed no emotion as Cindy spoke. She had known for years that Cindy adored Blaine and had a crush on him since the day she met him. Hearing Cindy's account of Blaine's treatment of her and the other girls only reaffirmed her belief in him. The bartender brought the soda and a glass of ice over to the table. She was about twenty-seven years old, a six-foot beauty, very slender with enormous breasts. She had a dark Gothic look. Black hair, lips, nails, colorful tattoos, and an array of body piercings. She haunted Jessica with her deep, dark eyes. It was an eerie stare meant to intimidate Jessica, letting her know that her presence was unwanted. She walked back to the bar with a beverage tray in hand. Jessica sensed she'd met the woman before but couldn't remember where.

"Who is that?" Jessica asked.

"Oh, that's Erin. She's new. She has no family here in town, and she said she needed a job in the worst way, so I hired her. She's a pretty good bartender, and she works for the low."

"How long has she been working for you?"

"She's been here for about a couple of months."

"What's her story?"

"Well, she says she's here to attend school. She needed to make some cash to get food and other necessities. She practically got on her hands and knees, begging for work. I couldn't use her in the shows due to all the body art and her lack of experience. But I'm a sucker for a sad story. Especially if it involves women who are down on their luck. She's a pretty girl, though. I just gave her a try at the bar. She was a big hit with the men. My patrons think she's mysteriously sexy, and she rakes in the tips." While Cindy was still talking, Jessica left her seat and made her way to the bar. She took a seat on the bar stool and ordered a virgin bloody Mary.

"The bar's closed," Erin said to Jessica while cleaning whiskey glasses, not even looking up at her. "I'm not serving anybody until after six-thirty."

"I think it's okay for you to make an exception in this case," Jessica told her.

"As I said, the bar is closed, and we're not serving anybody until after six-thirty. What part of that did you not understand?"

"Well, I understand that if you don't make the drink, then Ms. Cindy may not like it, and you may lose your little job!" Erin looked up at Jessica with a fixed stare, making direct eye contact and trying to read her. She then looked over at Cindy. Cindy nodded her head, letting her know whatever Jessica wanted, she was to oblige.

"Fine!" Erin said, slamming the glass she was cleaning down on the counter. She gathered the ingredients, and with her back turned to Jessica, she began making the bloody Mary.

"So, I hear you're new in town; where are you from?"

"Look, you ordered a drink. That's my job, to fix you a drink. It's not mandatory that I answer any of your questions. Now, would you like Tabasco sauce in this?"

"No thank you," Jessica replied. Jessica left the drink on the bar and returned to the table where Cindy was seated.

"She has quite the attitude, huh?"

"Yeah, she's one tough cookie. I like that about her. You can't be a pushover in this business. These guys will chew you up and spit you out."

"Well, you should tell her to tone it down. I think she's a bit much. Just keep an eye on her. I'm outta here. I'll be in touch. Let me know if you hear anything I might find interesting."

"Will do."

Cindy walked towards the bar as Jessica made her way out of the club.

Jessica's phone rang as she was returning to her car. It was Marcus.

"Hey babe," Marcus said.

"Hi Marcus, what's going on with you?"

"I've been in meetings all day, and I returned to my hotel room to shower before dinner. When I turned on the TV, I saw a story about Blaine on the news. I heard something about the Scorned killings. What's going on there?" She breathed out slowly, exhausted by all the happenings of the last day and a half. She told Marcus everything.

"It's a big misunderstanding. They have the wrong guy. It'll be cleared up soon," she tells him.

"So, how are you doing, baby?"

"To tell you the truth, I'm a bit upset. I feel sorry for Blaine, and I'm concerned about him and those precious little boys of his. It just breaks my heart. He's more worried about them than himself."

"Is there anything I can do?"

"No," she said. "Thanks for asking."

"I'll be back in Arkansas in a couple of days. If you need me just call me."

"I thank you for the kind gesture, Marcus. I'll be alright."

"I'm just letting you know, just in case. I'll talk with you later," he said.

"Okay, bye." Jessica got in her car and drove home. She was exhausted already, and the day was only half over. She went inside and threw her car keys on the kitchen counter, grabbed a glass from the cabinet, poured vodka in it, and then checked her messages. Among the many messages, there was one from Detective Armstrong.

"Hey Barnes, give me a call when you get this message; I may have some news for ya." She returned his call. He picked up on the first ring.

"Yeah Armstrong, what's up?"

"Hey Barnes, guess what I found out today?"

"What's that?"

"I called in a favor and I had the official toxicology reports done on Blaine and guess what they found? Roofies. Also, the shirt he was wearing the morning we found him was tested. It contained vomit, sweat and it had traces of the drug." Jessica had a look of relief on her face. She let out a deep sigh.

"So, he *was* drugged. Just as I suspected. Now we need to go back and question everyone at that pub and see just how the drug got into his system."

"I'm already on it," Detective Armstrong said.

"I'll meet you down there." She got her keys and headed to the downtown pub. Detective Armstrong was already there, waiting in his car. They both went inside. They walked to the bar and grabbed a seat. A male bartender greeted them and asked,

"What can I get you?"

"I'd like to speak to the manager," said Detective Armstrong.

"Well, you're talking to him." The medium build white man from behind the bar appeared to be in his early sixties. Jessica could tell he was wearing a toupee because the color of what was supposed to be black was slightly off from his naturally greying hair. "I own this place, and it looks as if I'm the bartender this evening. The guy I hired quit on me yesterday. It's hard to find good help these days. The guy wasn't on the job a good two months before he just up and quit on me out of the blue. He didn't even stick around for his paycheck. I had two of'em to quit. It's a damn shame. I would've liked for the girl to stick around. I couldn't keep the guys away from the bar. She dressed a little weird, though. Looked like a vampire or something, but she sure had a nice rack on her."

"Was she about five-eleven or so?" Jessica asked.

"Yeah, very pretty girl if she didn't wear all that black shit on her face."

"Is her name Erin?"

"No, her name is Nita."

"What was the name of the guy who quit on you?"

"Hey, why all the interest?" Detective Armstrong flashed his badge.

"I'm Detective Byron Armstrong with the Little Rock Police Department's homicide division. We're investigating a death. That's the interest."

"So, what brings you here? There was no murder committed here."

"No, there wasn't. We just wanted to ask you a few questions about everyone who had access to fixing drinks for your patrons this week."

"So, what do you think happened?" he asked curiously.

"That's what we're trying to find out."

"Well, Art, you know the guy who quit."

"What's Art's full name?" Detective Armstrong asked.

"Arthur Manchester. I hired him about a couple of months ago as a manager. He seemed like a pretty stand-up fella. He was a funny guy and very talkative. I liked him a lot. I hate he left. He kept the mood light around here. The employees liked him, and he was good with the customers. I hadn't had a single call-in from the employees while he was manager. They enjoyed working for him. He lightened my load, and I was able to concentrate on other things that needed my attention."

"When did you hire, the girl?" Jessica asked.

"Oh, I didn't hire her, Art did." Jessica looked at Armstrong and she looked back at the owner of the club.

"Arthur hired her?"

"Yep," he replied, looking curious.

"Who else did he hire?" Jessica asked.

"Just the girl."

"Did he have to run it by you before he hired anybody?" Detective Armstrong asked.

"Yes he did, but she came cheap, so I didn't mind him hiring her."

He called over an employee to man the bar while he took them to his office. He gave them all the information they requested of him, and they left. Detective Armstrong stepped outside and made a phone call to the police department and had them run the information that the owner had given them, but nothing was found. Art and Nita used fictitious names and social security numbers. The pub owner gave Detective Armstrong a few items that Art would have used during his employment, like ink pens and ledgers or anything else in the office that may have contained his fingerprints. While he was doing that, Jessica was piecing together the information in her mind that the owner had given them about the tattooed girl. She met Detective Armstrong outside of the bar. She said,

"I think I know where the girl is. If this is the same girl, then she's going by the name Erin. She's over at Cindy's working now even as we speak. I'm going to head back over there right now. I need you to meet me there." Jessica hurried over to Cindy's club. By then, the place was packed with customers, and she could barely get through the door. She squeezed in among the patrons and made her way to the bar looking for Cindy. A few female bartenders were working but she didn't see Erin. A brunette bartender asked,

"What can I get you?"

"I need to see Cindy. Is she around?"

"Yep, she's in her office in the back. I'll send for her," the young lady said. As the bartender walked away, Jessica turned around to look over the club. The upper echelon of party goers and a host of other patrons both male and female flooded the place. Go-go dancers were perched on swings above everyone else while some were behind walls of glass. Beautiful women of all nationalities were serving tables and tending the bar. They resembled models from the famous mansion. In addition, there were handsome men with bulging muscles waiting tables for the ladies or anyone who requested them. Speaking under her breath, Jessica said, *"Looks like a busy night for Cindy. She must be enjoying this."* As she continued looking around the club, she saw everyone dressed in their most expensive and classy attire. She looked down at her clothing. She was wearing tan slacks and a tank top with gym shoes. Feeling underdressed, she was tempted to let her hair down to look a little more presentable. She's beautiful so she didn't need to do much, but she felt a little out of place. Reminding herself of her real purpose, she didn't give it another thought. Finally, Cindy walked in.

"Hey Jessica. What brings you back so soon?"

"I need to talk to you."

"Sure," Cindy said. "Come on back to my office where it's a little quieter." They went to Cindy's office and engaged in small talk.

"I can't remember seeing a crowd as large as tonight's."

"That's probably because my shows are a little more risqué. I mean, I'm really pushing the envelope. Sensual erotica with a hint of romance sells. It's not so taboo anymore. That's why I opened this place. Did you know that women patrons make up a large percentage of my customers? They come in with their husbands or girlfriends. Most come alone. I've sprinkled a little handsome eye candy around for them. I notice you and your handsome young man out in the audience sometimes."

"Yeah, we love the shows, but the food is what brings us by so often. That new chef of yours can really cook. He's earned those five stars. I'm so proud of you. You've come a long way, girly. You pulled yourself up by your bootstraps and got your life back on track. I can remember the not-so-good days."

"Hey, I had to find my niche in life. I got clean, paid my way through school, and got my degree. I took what I knew about this industry, my love of poetry, and made it work for me. I've even ventured out into other areas and made some sound financial investments, and I'm doing well now. Who knew that I could make a career out of this and do it legally and get a lot of girls off the streets in the process? Did you know that all the girls who work for me must be clean and must submit themselves to a drug test before I allow them to work? Druggies don't have a good work ethic, and they compromise themselves and my business. I run a very strict and professional place, and anyone caught compromising it is quickly terminated. I'll help you if you want my help, but if you fuck up with me, it's your ass. I don't have time for a bunch of bullshit in my place. Besides, our city has gotten stricter codes that I refuse to violate. I've worked too hard to be here, and I'm not about to let anyone fuck that up."

"I hear you!" Jessica said. She hurried to her topic.

"Cindy, I came by to ask you about the bartender that you hired, Erin. Is she still here?"

"She said she wasn't feeling well and she needed to take the evening off, so I let her go home."

"Do you have an address or a phone number for her?"

"Yes, I have a cell phone number for her. Why?"

"I need to ask her a few questions." At that moment, a young lady came in and announced to Cindy that Detective Armstrong was there to see her.

"Send him on back." Detective Armstrong came and met them in the office. Cindy looked at Jessica out of curiosity. "What's going on, Jessica? What's with the police visit?"

"He just wants to ask Erin some questions."

"About what? Is she in some kind of trouble?"

"She may be a witness, and we really need to speak with her. Can you get me the number?"

"Sure, Jessica." Cindy went over to her desk, looked through her book of numbers, and wrote the number down for her. "Here it is, right here." Cindy handed her the number. "If I need her to cover someone's shift, I use this number."

"Look Cindy, I don't want to spook her, so I'm going to get you to call her for me. See if you can get her to meet you here, but don't tell her that we want to talk with her." Jessica handed Cindy the number back. She sat at her desk and made the call but got no answer. Cindy left a message on her voicemail pretending to need to talk about some inventory concerning the bar.

"Well, as you can see, no answer. So, are you going to tell me what this is about?"

"I'm not sure yet, but I'll let you know something later. If she contacts you, call us quickly. Oh, Cindy do you happen to have video surveillance in the club?"

"I sure do, I wouldn't be caught dead without it. Of course, my employees don't know that we have them. It's my way of weeding out the bad and keeping the good. The camera doesn't lie."

Detective Armstrong asked, "Would you be willing to let us take a look at the tape?"

"Yes, I sure will, but it's not a tape it's a digital recording."

"Who monitors your system? Do you have a security company monitoring your cameras?"

"Yes, and I can monitor them from here or by phone or laptop. I can see what's going on from anywhere in the world. All I have to do is log into my account. I have the cameras in the front and back parking lot as well as inside. The security company installed the surveillance system so well that nobody knows the cameras are here, and that's the way I want it"

Cindy powered up her computer, logged into her security system, and gave them access.

"Cindy, did Erin ever have any visitors here at the club, and if so, how frequent?"

"She had a guy come by a couple of times to pick her up. I don't know how she got home this evening, but you can look at the camera and see. It records everything for up to two years and she's only been working here for a couple of months. If you want, you can make a copy by placing a thumb drive in the computer. I have a few in my desk drawer if you need one." Jessica walked over to Cindy and kissed her on the cheek.

"Cindy, did I tell you how crazy I am about you?"

"Yeah, yeah, you scratch my back, and I scratch yours. I know how this works." Cindy looked at Detective Armstrong. You know all of this comes at a price for you, don't you?"

Detective Armstrong flashed a flirty smile. With a light brush of his hand on her cheek, he said, "Yeah, put it on my tab sweetheart!"

"Oh no, you think you're cute but it's going to cost you extra for flirting! And you're a married man. I don't know where you got your information, but I ain't that type of girl, sweetie." Cindy laughed and lightly smacked him on his ass.

"Let me know when you're done, Jessica. I'll be out here if you need me." Cindy left them in her office and went back into the club. Jessica and Detective Armstrong continued studying the video. They saw plenty of footage that included Erin and what seemed to be a tall top-heavy white guy with black hair. He was six foot two and about two hundred and ninety pounds. They recorded everything from the past three months. Armstrong took the video back to the precinct to view it. Jessica followed in her car. They studied the footage for about an hour.

"Barnes, it's getting a little late. You've been at it all day. Don't you think you need to go home and get some rest? I'll get this video to the right people and have them sort through the footage we don't need, and we can continue this tomorrow okay."

Jessica exhaled and said, "I suppose you're right. It's going on eleven o'clock. I wasn't paying attention to the time. I'll talk with you tomorrow." He walked her to her vehicle, where they shared a little small talk, and she left.

CHAPTER THREE

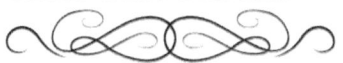

Jessica pulled her car into the driveway. She noticed a suspicious car parked there. *"Now, who in the hell is here this time of night?"* She snapped her gun out of its holster and turned on her high beams. She opened her car door and positioned herself with the door partially covering her body for protection. She held her gun to her side, ready to fire. A shadowy figure came out from the darkness and walked towards her car.

"Hold it right there!" she demanded. The person stopped suddenly.

"It's me, baby," the male voice shouted from the darkness. Jessica recognized the voice. She began putting her gun back in its holster.

"Marcus, what are you doing here? I didn't think you'd be back for a couple of days." He walked over to her car.

"I was about to shoot the shit outta you," she said.

"Why didn't you call to let me know you'd be back in town?"

"I wanted to surprise you, baby," Marcus said as he kissed her.

"Yeah, and you almost got shot in the process."

"Oh baby, you weren't really going to shoot me, were you?" Marcus kissed her again. He handed her a single red rose.

"Hell yeah. You know I'm trigger-happy this time of night, and you're driving a rental too. You know you can't do that to me." He continued kissing her covering her mouth with his lips as she was trying to scold him. His kisses calmed her. She was secretly happy to see him. His presence was a welcome surprise, and she needed him that night, especially with everything she'd gone through. He hopped in her vehicle and properly parked it while she unlocked the door to her place. He followed her inside and locked the door behind him. He went into the kitchen and fixed her a glass of vodka on the rocks and one for himself and added a little cranberry juice.

"You know, I finished early, and I decided to come back tonight. I caught the first flight out." He handed her the drink as he sat on the sofa. She took a sip. "That's just how I like it; straight." He took a seat beside her, placed his drink on the table, and motioned for her to put her feet on his lap. After taking off her shoes he began massaging her feet. She needed it. Marcus was young, handsome, and very sexy. He's twenty-eight and she's forty-two. Jessica loved their arrangement. He was the only guy who seemed to understand her sexually and in many other ways as well. Because of the large age gap, she knew there couldn't be anything more than a friendship and their mutual sexual arrangement. Besides, she wasn't ready for anything more than that, regardless of age.

Marcus continued rubbing her feet. She relaxed pressing her body into the sofa.

"Marcus, why does it seem as if you always know what's best for me?"

"That's because I fit you. We were made for each other."

"Oh, stop it with that," she said. They finished their drinks and talked a little more. Jessica went into her bathroom to shower. Marcus fixed them another round of drinks and took them to her bedroom. As she showered, she allowed the events of the day to run through her mind. She began thinking about Blaine. She wanted so desperately to help him. She was sure of his innocence, and she felt bad for every moment he had to spend in jail and there was little she could do. Pushing her head under the flow of the shower she let the hot water run through her hair. With her eyes closed, she placed her hands on the wall and breathed air into her lungs. She felt Marcus' hands on her waist as he kissed the back of her neck. She exhaled slowly and breathed in as he pressed his body into hers. She felt his member rubbing across her ass. She was instantly turned on. He turned her towards him and began to passionately kiss her feeding her his tongue as she greedily accepted. He kissed her on the neck and moved his way down to her breast. Her heart began to race, and her breathing escalated as he gently placed her breast into his mouth feverishly sucking her nipples. Her knees became weak, and she fell into his arms. He held her up and quickly grabbed her towel hanging over the shower rod. He wrapped the towel around her body and led her to the bedroom. With her body still wet he dried her as she lay motionless in the bed. He then took her towel, dried himself, and wrapped it around his waist. He got her drink and handed it to her.

He took a sip of his drink. As he stood at the foot of her bed, he let the towel drop to the floor. Jessica couldn't help but look. She loved looking at his body. He was well-built. His daily workouts paid off handsomely in the form of the body of a Greek god. He stood still to allow her to admire his body and smiled. She returned the smile.

"Come here Adonis," she said playfully. He took her drink from her hand and placed it on the nightstand. He slowly inched in closer leaning over the bed. He took her by the waist and gently pulled her body to the edge of the bed. Taking her right leg, he began kissing and massaging her feet. She was getting excited as he licked her toes. She pulled her leg back slightly as the sensation caused an instant reflex. He continued playfully. She begged for him as she saw him getting excited. He shook his head no. He was determined to love every inch of her body completely. He dropped to his knees and pulled her hips to the edge of the bed. He kissed her inner thighs, and he loved her sweetness with his mouth until she exploded with the force of a tidal wave. She pressed her hips against his mouth and screamed with delight as she released her nectar, and he sucked it all in. She loves it when he loves her in this way. She's never had anyone to love her body like this young man. She was addicted to him. She wouldn't dare tell him she simply took advantage of the opportunity.

He wants her for himself and will stop at nothing to get her. He's mesmerized by her, and he tells himself that he's going to make her his wife if it's the last thing he does. When loving her he holds nothing back. He pours himself into their lovemaking with every ounce of his being. He continues sucking, pulling, and tasting her until she lies there motionless. He slowly moved up and lifted her body gently pushing her toward the head of the bed. He then placed himself inside her. He pumps her with as much force as a locomotive. She comes alive as he grinds her rapidly. She gripped his firm buttocks and pulled him deeper inside her. She felt a sensation of floating from her body as she arched her back and gripped him so that he could meet her as she gave him her all. He was becoming excited by her reaction, and he released his spirit into her, emptying his young, hot love deep inside her, causing him to want her even more. She pulled him close and passionately kissed him. The warmth of his body and his massive size excited her. She felt protected, loved, wanted, and needed. For a brief moment, she imagined that he was all hers and that she loved him and he her. He was a willing participant. He longed to give her everything she wanted, and he would meet any need, all she needed to do was ask. She allowed this to play in her mind as she held him tight. He was amazed at the passion she was expressing, and he enjoyed every moment. He could tell her feelings were deeper than she let on and was taken aback, especially since she constantly reminded him that they could be nothing more than friends with benefits. He didn't ask any questions; he simply enjoyed his time with her. He lay on his side, pulled her body close to his, and held her, stroking her body. She exhaled. "Damn Marcus, you were great! I can hardly keep up with your young ass." He kissed her ear and whispered.

"You can handle me."

She lay there with a million thoughts running through her head: thoughts of Blaine and the boys and then back to Marcus. She could feel herself getting attached to Marcus. She found that she needed him more and she was no longer feeling that his lingering presence was as annoying as in the beginning. Lately, he had been allowed to stay over more often and much later than usual even spending the weekend together. Her day had been stressful, and he had managed to ease a great deal of it away. He did everything to make her happy. Since she wasn't big on having a maid service in her home, Marcus took it upon himself to lighten her load by having her vehicles cleaned and fueled weekly and helping her out around the home in any way she needed. Although Jessica is very wealthy, he's still a gentleman who loves to shower her with gifts, cash, or anything else he knows she loves. Being with a powerful woman like Jessica who already seemed to have everything, he pulled out all the stops to impress her.

After noticing her reaction to him Marcus thought, *"Perhaps I'm making progress. She was happy to see me tonight."* He knew she loved having him over for sex, but it was at her discretion. Although she was kind to him, she'd never shown any signs of being in love with him. She was tough and hard to discern. She didn't wear her emotions on her sleeves so he could never really tell what she was thinking.

Jessica and Marcus met at a charity event. Both are avid bikers so when the local chapter of black professional bikers teamed up to provide for the needy foster kids, they both attended. He noticed her standing by her bike talking with a few of her associates. He thought she was beautiful, so he went out of his way to *accidentally* bump into her. He also liked her bike. It was an orange custom-made tricked-out crotch rocket. Pretty impressive for a lady rider he had to admit. They chatted for a while. Jessica learned that he worked for the largest investment firm in the state of Arkansas and had obtained a great deal of wealth not only for his clients but for himself as well. Jessica was impressed at all he'd managed to accomplish at such a young age. His firm handled a few of her father's investments too. After small talk, they exchanged information for the sake of business according to him. He called and the conversation went from investments to bikes and so on. He asked if they could ride together. She accepted the offer. Besides being handsome and accomplished, she noticed his charming personality and great sense of humor. He was also mature for his age. After a couple of months of trying to persuade her to date him, she finally agreed. They've been seeing each other ever since. She says he just kind of grew on her. Although Jessica feels he's a great guy, she had her reasons for not pursuing a serious relationship. She felt that a young handsome guy like Marcus needed to keep his options open and find a young woman his age. At the least, he could get married and have children. She didn't want him to destroy his chances of living a fulfilling life.

He's not interested in women his age. His reasons were that most young women were indecisive or insecure. His statement to that is, *"They put your balls in a vice to control you. It's a smothering effect that I hate."* It wasn't that way with Jessica. He was free with her. She put no stress or demands on him. She's sure of herself and lives in her own world and her confidence is unwavering. This made her even more irresistible to him. She's smart and beautiful, and a great lover. He longs to be more than friends, but he doesn't press the issue. He accepts her terms and continues with the hope that she'll change her mind. Jessica turned towards him and their eyes met.

"I'm glad you're here." She laid her head on his massive chest and closed her eyes. He looked down at her, pulled her hair from her face, and smiled.

"Jessie, baby, did you eat today?"

"I had a bagel and some other junk, why do you ask?"

"Because I know that sometimes you don't eat right as you should."

"Oh, I'll be alright. It's only one day, and besides with all that's going on, I don't have much of an appetite."

"I think you need to eat something."

"I'm okay Marcus," she mumbled and kissed his chest.

"Let me make you a little snack," he said.

"It's too late to eat now."

He kissed her forehead and said, "I have to use the restroom. I'll be back." He went to the restroom and freshened up. He then went into the kitchen, opened a can of clam chowder, warmed it, made a turkey and cheese sandwich, and took it to the bedroom. He placed the food on the nightstand.

"Jessie, wake up honey." She opened her eyes and looked up at him. She sat up in bed.

"Boy, what have you done?"

"Go ahead. Eat."

"Marcus, you didn't have to do this." He handed her the plate with the bowl of soup and sandwich.

"You may as well grab the other half of this sandwich because I'm not going to be able to eat all of it."

"You don't have to eat it all, but you do need to eat something." She looked at him and smiled.

"What am I going to do with you?"

"I could think of a few things," he replied taking the other half of the sandwich from the plate.

"Yeah, I just bet you can with your mannish ass," she said pushing at him playfully. They finished eating and made love again, and she fell asleep in his arms.

The next morning, Marcus put on a pot of coffee and showered while Jessica slept. It was nine o'clock. He poured her a cup and took it to her.

"Hey babe," he said waking her. She woke up and took the coffee.

"Wow, you're up and at it this morning. What time is it?"

"It's around nine." She sipped her coffee.

"Are you headed to the office?"

"I have a few meetings and then I'm free the rest of the day, you have something in mind?"

"Not today. I have a lot to do, but I'll call you later," she told him. They talked a little more about their plans, and Marcus got his things and left.

Jessica got out of bed and checked her voicemail. No messages. She showered, got dressed, and sat at the edge of her bed while putting her gun in the holster. She looked over at the nightstand and noticed that Marcus had left his watch. She leaned back and picked it up. She held it in her hands and smiled, wishing she was still in his arms. *"Get it together girl, you're letting this young dick go to your head."* She realized that she was becoming closer to him, more than she allowed herself to believe. She returned the watch to the nightstand, got her keys and cell phone, and left. She called Detective Armstrong and left a message for him. She drove over to the county jail to visit Blaine

The guards escorted him into the visitation booth. She noticed he was growing stubble, and he looked drained. He didn't look like the same person. He slumped down in his seat like a zombie, and he slowly looked up at Jessica.

"Hi Blaine," she said trying to give him a warm friendly smile. She could tell by his facial expression he wasn't doing well. "How are you doing? You hanging in there?"

"About as much as can be expected given the circumstances," he said.

"Your toxicology report came back positive for Rohypnol. We're investigating a couple of suspicious characters who worked at the bar you visited on the night in question. The only thing that ties you to this case is that you were in the car with Ms. Jackson. Trust me, Blaine. Armstrong and I are doing everything we can. The more we investigate, the clearer it becomes that you're being framed, and I'm going to catch the assholes that set you up. Everybody knows that you're innocent, and we're going to prove it. All I need for you to do is hang in there, be strong, and we'll have you out of here in no time."

"Jessica, please hurry. I don't think I can take another day in lock-up."

"Don't worry. I just need you to hold on a few more days, and we'll get you out of here. I promise you that!" He looked away, not wanting any more delays. A few more days would seem like a lifetime. "Look at me, Blaine. You need to be strong right now. You can't be in here falling apart and shit. I need you to have patience, and you'll be with your boys in no time." Jessica knew that Blaine was not upset for himself but for his children. In their many years of friendship, she'd never seen him so distraught.

He's a strong man and can withstand anything and has endured his share of hardships, from being raised by a single mom and standing in his dad's place to serving in the war to being shot by a gang lord on the violent streets of Little Rock in the height of its gang wars. He has seen it all. But being away from his sons was killing him. He couldn't bear another day without them.

"Armstrong will present his latest findings to the prosecuting attorney. Hopefully, they'll get you back in to see the judge with the new evidence, so you can at least make bond until you're exonerated. So, bear with us. There's nothing that ties you to the death of Chief Albright's daughter although some are trying to speculate you may have had something to do with it. Somebody's trying to throw the attention from themselves by casting a cloud of suspicion over you.

"Jessica, I appreciate everything you're doing for me," he said, pretending to be strong. They talked until the guard arrived, signaling the visit was over. He escorted Blaine back to his cell. Jessica's heart was broken for her friend, which only fueled her passion all the more to clear his name. She left the jail and called Detective Armstrong to see if he had heard anything on the surveillance video but still no answer. She went to see Karen Reed, Blaine's attorney. Once there, they discussed Blaine's case and the possibility of new evidence to see how soon she could petition the court to get another hearing. His attorney reassured her that she knew the judge personally and she would discuss the case with her. While leaving the attorney's office, Detective Armstrong called.

"Yeah, Barnes here."

"Hey Barnes, I need to see you fast."

"What is it?"

"You're not going to believe what we found. Get your ass over here now!" She zipped through traffic like a rocket. Once she arrived at the precinct, they went into his office, and he closed his door for more privacy.

"Barnes, we found an abandoned cab at a truck stop in North Little Rock. There was no way to tell who the driver was because the suspect did a great job of covering his face, but he left identifiable prints. The taxicab had been reported stolen. When we searched it, we found evidence of a struggle. We think the murder may have taken place in the taxicab because we found Ms. Jackson's DNA there.

Hair samples and her fingerprints were everywhere. The cab was ransacked. With all of that struggling, you would think that we would've found some of Blaine's DNA on the victim, but the lab has turned up nothing. If Blaine didn't killed her, the real killer may have placed the dead girl and Blaine in the back seat of his car. Also, the crime lab didn't find any evidence linking Blaine to Lana Albright's death."

"Wow, that sounds like it could be great news for Blaine."

"That's not all; take a look at what we have."

They went through the surveillance footage, which had been narrowed down to the male and female subjects. They watched the suspects in question come and go freely.

"There's Erin right there," Jessica pointed out the female bartender on the camera working at the bar. They saw a white male coming over to the bar and talking with her on several different days as well as in the parking lot. Both of them could be seen getting in and out of what appeared to be a white late-model Cadillac.

"That's going to be our guy right there," Detective Armstrong said, pointing at the man. There's plenty of footage with the two of them together. At times, they can be seen arguing in the parking lot. Armstrong, fast-forwarding the video up to Jessica's visit, said,

"Now, here's what I wanted you to see."

They took a closer look. Jessica saw herself on the screen. She could be seen walking to the bar where Erin was standing. While Jessica was talking to her, Erin turned her back to her, and from the angle of the camera, she could be seen pulling a tiny vial from her bosom and emptying its contents into the drink that she prepared for her. Jessica looked on in anger, "That dirty bitch! And to think I almost drank that shit. I know she's the one who drugged Blaine." Erin could be seen making a phone call immediately after Jessica had spoken with her at the bar. After the phone call, the male subject picked her up and they left the property.

Still photos were taken from the footage and placed into the criminal database to determine the proper identities of the two suspects, along with the fingerprint evidence obtained from the pub owner. Hits came back immediately for the female Erin Rogers, twenty-seven years old, from Baton Rouge. She had misdemeanor crimes she'd committed between the ages of fifteen to seventeen. She had been a ward of the state and a known runaway. She had a few shoplifting charges but no major crimes. The guy's name is Arthur Manley. He served time in a Louisiana prison for manslaughter and was released after serving ten years. He killed a guy during a fight that the victim supposedly instigated. According to his parole, he's not supposed to be out of the state of Louisiana.

Detective Armstrong got the license plate number from the car and immediately put out a BOLO for them.

"I'm going to get out of here," Jessica told the detective. "I have to get back with Blaine's attorney and let her know what we have."

"How's he doing?"

"Not well," she said with a temporary blank stare.

"We've got to get him out of there. I wish you would visit him, Armstrong, he needs that. He needs all of the support he can get."

"I'll go by there as soon as I get a break. Hopefully, we can come up with something today on these two suspects and perhaps bring them in for questioning. It seems there's a chance we may be able to exclude Blaine as a suspect. At least with these two suspicious characters, there's hope," he said looking at the computer screen. "Let's keep our fingers crossed. I'm going to take these photos and show them to the owner and the employees at the pub and if they can identify them as the two that worked there, we'll have more to go into court with."

"Okay, sounds good. Well, I'm out of here, call me if you hear something okay." Jessica left the precinct to see Blaine's attorney.

The Hearing

Blaine and his attorney were allowed to view the new evidence. Blaine recognized Erin and Arthur as bartenders in the pub. He recalled how close they appeared to be. Arthur was the guy who called the cab for Blaine, and Erin was the one who'd served the opened bottles of beer. The pub's owner confirmed that Erin and Arthur worked for him, and they were both on duty the night that Blaine was there. When the video was shown in court of Erin fixing Jessica's drink at Cindy's club, she could clearly be seen putting a foreign substance in the drink. They called a few other witnesses to court. After presenting their latest findings to the prosecuting attorney's office, another bond hearing was granted. Since Blaine was found inside the vehicle in a compromising position, the charges wouldn't be officially dropped until the investigation was complete. The prosecuting attorney presented the argument that Blaine should be required to wear an electronic monitoring device as a condition of his release. However, the judge decided against it, and Blaine was released on bond pending the outcome of the case. Jessica took him to his ex-wife's home to visit the children. She was expecting him. Sheila made a meal for them. They talked about everything other than the case. They ate and Blaine enjoyed his children. The kids knew nothing about the case because their mom had shielded them from it. Jessica, happy that her friend was out of jail, was exhausted and ready to go home. She motioned for Blaine to meet her outdoors. "Sheila, I'm leaving now. I must get some rest. It's been an exciting evening." Jessica said her goodbyes to the children, Sheila and her fiancé Virgil. She and Blaine walked outside to the carport.

"Blaine, I know you're not ready to leave but we have to go. What do you want to do? Do you think she would allow the boys to go home with you and spend the night?"

"Give me a few more minutes, and let me say good night to them, and I'll be ready, okay." Jessica agreed. Afterward, they went back to her place. She prepared the spare bedroom for him and made him a drink. After discussing the case, they both went to bed.

The following morning, Blaine woke to the smell of fresh coffee and bacon. There was more food cooking, but the bacon and the coffee permeated the air as if they were in competition with each other. He smiled as he lay on his back looking at the ceiling for a moment. Happy to be free, he thought about all he needed to get done for the day. He planned to rent a car because his car was still being held at the police impound as evidence. He also needed to find temporary shelter because his home was still off-limits to him. He wanted to try to get back into a routine so he could maintain a sense of normalcy. He heard his name being called.

"Blaine, breakfast!" Jessica yelled.

"Okay, I'll be out in a minute."

Jessica was sitting at the table when Blaine came in. She was sipping coffee and reading the local newspaper.

"Morning," Jessica said as Blaine walked past her to pour himself a cup of coffee.

"This definitely is not jail food," he said looking at the spread that Jessica had laid out for him. "Waffles, bacon, ham, eggs, and grits with cheese and a large pot of freshly brewed coffee. Girl, you really know me don't you"

"I thought that you could use a change from jail food."

"I didn't eat while I was there," Blaine said as he stuffed a slice of bacon in his mouth. He fixed his plate and took a seat across from Jessica. "Any good news in there?"

"Bad news this morning. You may as well know that your story is all over the news and on the internet front page. Also, there are several reporters outside waiting for you to come out. Channel Nine called asking for an exclusive story. I referred them to your attorney. I don't have to tell you how to handle the press. I'm just ready for your name to be cleared and for all this mess to be over with so that things can get back to normal. I know Sheila has her hands full trying to protect the boys from all the media drama. You'll have to do the same. Do you want to continue staying on here with me until all of this is over, or do you want to get a hotel room?"

"I was thinking about that earlier. I love you Jessie, and I thank you for everything you're doing for me, but I think it would be better if I got a hotel room. I can get one of those suites with a kitchenette. Besides, I don't want to intrude on your space."

"You won't be intruding. I would love to have you here. You know that."

"Yeah, but as long as I'm here, the press will be here hounding you and you don't need that."

"Blaine, I think I can handle them but do what you feel is best."

"They should be finished processing my place in a few more days. I should be able to go home soon, but I will need a ride to pick up a rental car today," Blaine said finishing his last bite of waffles. "I'll be ready after I get a quick shower."

"I'm ready when you are," she said.

CHAPTER FOUR

At the corner of Baseline and Geyer Springs Road, Erin was sitting in the car waiting for Arthur to come out of the store. She was very anxious. She was upset about having to leave town again. Arthur jumped in the car. He was on the phone with his boss. He had been paid to drug Blaine. He thought it would be an easy job. He didn't think anything of it until he realized that Blaine was a former police officer. Since his time in prison, he had been out doing odd jobs trying to go straight. He met Erin while in Baton Rouge. They hit it off immediately and he felt they made a great team. Arthur is ten years older than Erin. Since she grew up in foster care, she had been a ward of the state without a father or mother, he was like a father figure to her. He liked her attitude and her willingness to do anything needed to survive. She was tough, strong, and very opinionated. She was also very loyal.

Arthur was trying to concentrate on his phone call while Erin was in the background yelling at him. She knew the police were on their trail, but he needed the cash that had been promised him by the boss so they could leave town immediately. Erin didn't know who Arthur was doing the job for and she didn't know why they were being paid to set up Blaine until they saw it on the news. She began to wonder if it had anything to do with the murders. She was the one who fixed the drinks while Arthur did whatever he was paid to do. She didn't exactly know what his role was. She had questions and she wanted answers. She didn't mind an occasional scam here and there and Arthur was the best at it. His scams always netted tons of money which they would have enough to live on comfortably for six to eight months. As long as nobody got hurt, she was all for it. He ended his call with the boss, and Erin yelled,

"I'm not going down for murder Art! What the fuck's going on? Did you kill all those women?"

Arthur didn't speak verbally; he simply shook his head. Frustrated with him for not answering her question, she asked, "Are you the Scorned killer?"

"Calm down Erin. I didn't kill anybody. Remember I was there with you. How could I have murdered anybody? You know that's not how we operate. Now listen to me. As soon as the boss calls back, we'll meet the delivery guy, and we'll have our money and skip this fucking city. Shit, we'll be long gone from this place in just a few hours. While he was still talking, his cell phone rang again. It was the boss, and they were to meet a drop-off guy at their normal meeting spot at a local burger joint on the outskirts of town. They got their money and quickly left town.

In the meantime, Blaine's home was returned to him, and he was settling in. He tried going back to work and getting on with his life as usual, but a cloud of suspicion still loomed over him and faint whispers followed him everywhere he went. He decided to lay low for a while and spend most of his time with his sons. Detective Armstrong was still trying to track Arthur and Erin to no avail. They were also investigating the other murders, trying to clear Blaine of all suspicion but for the most part, they were unable to find any more clues to rule him out as a suspect.

Jessica was working on Blaine's case as much as she could, but she had other clients who needed her attention, so she worked on what she was able to do until something new came down the wire. She knew Blaine had been lying low, so she wanted to treat him to dinner. She called to set up plans and invited him to dine with her. He agreed and they met at a local restaurant well known for its steaks.

Besides Cindy's place, it was another one of their favorite steak houses out in West Little Rock.

Jessica was having a glass of wine at the bar when Blaine showed up about twenty minutes late. She watched as he stumbled up the steep stairway. He appeared to be intoxicated. She stood at her feet when she saw him make his way inside the large glass double doors. She beckoned for him to come towards her. She met him and they were escorted to their table in the dining area. They were seated and given menus. She studied him for a second and asked, "Long day?"

"You could say that," he said with slurred speech.

"Would you like to tell me about it?"

"Not really, but since you asked, I feel as if I'm living my life in a bubble. I can't take the negative publicity and horrid stares from people who recognize me from the news. You ought to see the dirty looks I get when I'm out with my sons at local parks. People are grabbing their loved ones to protect them from me. Here I am trying to protect my family, and people treat me as if I were a monster or deviant like the ones we used to fight against.

After I dropped the boys off today, Sheila hit me with some news I couldn't handle too well."

"What was the news?"

"She's suggesting that I minimize my visits with the boys until all of this blows over. She says it's to protect them, but I can't be away from my children."

"I understand Sheila's point, but I believe that you two can come up with an arrangement that will better suit you and the children."

"She and Virgil seem to have already made their minds up about it. I'm cool with him, and he seems to show great interest when it comes to my boys, but they're still my children, and I don't feel it's his place to tell me what I can and can't do with my own children."

"Blaine, I believe they both have the boy's best interest at heart. I don't think it's personal. It's for their good. Perhaps they don't need to be in the spotlight. You know, there's always going to be that occasional reporter who's going to get a little too pushy to get the scoop and you don't want them getting caught up in that madness. You even mentioned that people are a bit skittish when they see you in public. You wouldn't want anyone to accost you while they're around, would you?"

"When I'm with my children, they ask me to take them places, and as their father, I hate telling them no. When Sheila and I divorced, we vowed we'd do everything we could to make the transition easier for them. We have managed to co-parent together without any issues. Now, I admit this is a hell of a situation we have on our hands, but I'm sure we can work something out. Virgil is suggesting no contact, but Sheila is saying we can visit in-house only and it's not a good idea to take them away from her home." Jessica listened as her friend poured out his feelings. Although she sympathized with Blaine, she couldn't help but agree with Sheila.

"I know it's upsetting news Blaine, but this will blow over real soon. The police will work it out. As you know, we have evidence you were drugged. Not only that, but we also saw the girl trying to drug me as well. All we have to do is catch up with them and find out what they know and figure out who's involved."

"I'll be glad when they catch those responsible because this is ruining my life. My children mean everything to me;

without them, my life has no meaning. They're the air I breathe and the reason I go on each day."

"Blaine, it's going to be okay," Jessica said comforting him. The server arrived at their table. They placed their order. Blaine ordered a glass of wine. Concerned for his well-being, Jessica asked, "How much have you had to drink today?"

"Nothing," he replied. She looked at him incredulously.

"Are you sure because, by the way you stumbled in here? I thought you were already a bit tipsy."

"Was I stumbling? I didn't notice it. I was with my children today. I don't drink around them. The only thing I had to drink today was iced tea that Shelia served during my visitation with her and Virgil."

"So, all you had to drink was tea?"

"Yeah" Feeling as though he was being interrogated, he asked, "What's with all the questions? You know, the last time I checked, I was still an adult. I don't need a babysitter. It seems that lately, everyone's been trying to run my life and tell me what I can and can't do. I'm a decent person, yet all of that has come into question. Everything I believe in and worked hard to maintain seems to be slipping through my fingers. You're treating me like a child. I tell you, Jessie, I don't need this right now, so spare me the crap and allow me to have one glass of wine with my damn steak. Is that too much to ask?"

She took a deep breath, slowly exhaled, and nodded her head, yes, knowing he was under a lot of pressure. He was upset with her, and she knew it. She chose not to take it personally. She produced a warm smile, one he was familiar with, and said, "Blaine, I apologize. I was looking out for you. I know you're going through a lot."

"No, I'm sorry, I'm a little frustrated. Sorry for snapping at you."

"You're good, let's just enjoy our meal."

She changed the subject. As much as Jessica tried to cheer him up, she could tell he was hurting. She didn't want him to be alone, so she suggested he spend the night at her place. He obliged. They played a game of dominoes and watched the latest cop shows on prime-time TV in which they both tried predicting the killers and solving the case. Afterward, Blaine went to bed.

Jessica lounged on the sofa. Her home phone rang. It was Marcus. She was glad to hear from him. After talking with him for the better part of an hour, they ended the call, and she, too, went to sleep.

Suspicious Activities

Blaine was heading to Sheila's home to pick up his children. After a heated discussion on the phone, she decided to allow them to leave with their father. More so because the children insisted on going. Blaine picked them up, and they went for pizza. Afterward, they rode go-karts and played a few games of laser tag, and video games until the boys were exhausted. He dropped them off and helped put them to bed. He talked with Sheila. After a while, Virgil, who had just come home, joined them. After a few awkward and uncomfortable minutes, Blaine left. He was sleepy, so he headed home.

On his way home, he noticed a vehicle in the middle of the road. The passenger side door was open. He pulled his vehicle behind the car. Acting on instinct, he went to investigate. He noticed a young white female as she lay slumped over the steering wheel. He couldn't see her face. Her long blonde hair was disheveled. He called out to her, "Ma'am, are you okay?" She slowly lifted her head. She appeared to be intoxicated. He opened the door, and she fell into his arms. He noticed blood pouring from a wound in her chest. She had been stabbed. He tried to revive her.

After no success, he called the paramedics and applied pressure to the wound. While he waited for the police and paramedics to arrive, he noticed signs of a struggle inside her car. She was wearing one shoe while the other was on the floor on the passenger side. The contents of her purse were strewn about, appearing as though she may have fought off her attacker with it. He noticed a box of Durex condoms, a rope, and other tell-tale signs that she was about to be victim number eight. She, too, was a local call girl. She didn't work the streets; she was a college student trying to pay her way through school. She had formerly worked for an escort agency disguised as such but was really a call-girl service. She felt she was giving too much of her profit away, so she decided to go out on her own working from her cell phone instead.

After a few minutes, the paramedics and the police arrived. The police questioned Blaine extensively. He told them everything he knew. It was like déjà vu. His clothing was taken; also, photos were taken of him, including his hands. His being found with the young lady cast an even greater cloud of suspicion over him, but he was allowed to go home pending the outcome of the investigation.

Whatever the young lady could tell them when she regained consciousness would determine whether he would be charged. He pulled into his driveway and sat in his car for a while, thinking about what he'd witnessed. He was startled when his cell phone rang, which was in his shirt pocket. It was Jessica.

"Blaine, what's going on over there? Are you okay?"

"Jessica, you wouldn't believe me if I told you."

"Armstrong told me what happened. It looks like the girl is going to recover. What I want to know is, how are you doing?"

"I really can't say right now because I'm in disbelief of what I just witnessed. This happens just as it seems things are going better for me. I don't know what it is about me, but I keep running into trouble that I'm not even a part of."

"When the girl wakes, she'll be able to tell the police who attacked her. In the meantime, you really need to lay low for a while. I'm headed over there now. I want to talk with you."

"Not tonight, Jessie; I'm not in the mood for talking. I just want to have a stiff drink and go to bed."

"Well, I'm coming anyway." He knew it was no use arguing with her, so he ended the call and went into the house. After he showered, he poured himself a drink and lay across his sofa. He had fallen asleep by the time Jessica made it. She let herself in with the spare key. She woke him and asked him to get into bed. Instead, he sat up and talked with her for a while. She spoke with him concerning all he had gone through. After talking to him for about an hour, he felt encouraged. He went to bed. She got a throw to cover her legs and watched TV until she fell asleep on the sofa.

She woke up early the next morning. Blaine was still asleep. She went to her car to get her bag so she could shower. She walked past Blaine's car and noticed something strange that caught her attention. She moved in for a closer look. There lying in his back seat was a cord of rope, a box of Durex condoms, a large knife that appeared to have dried blood on it and a pair of ladies' underwear. After running inside to get her cell phone, she went back to the car, opened the back door, and snapped a few pictures of the items, including the knife. She then went into Blaine's kitchen and looked at his knife block, compared it to the picture on her phone, and compared the knife to the other knives in the set. She was upset. She backed into the kitchen counter and gasped, *"Blaine, what's going on here? Are you an accomplice to murder?"* Her mind went racing while her heart was beating uncontrollably. She thought she would hit the floor as she lost feeling in her legs. *"Did I make the mistake of helping free a dangerous murderer?"* She went through Blaine's home, looking for more clues. She checked in on him. He was sound asleep. She continued her frantic search. After quickly scanning the place, she found nothing else. She sat back for a second while carefully considering the evidence. Blaine was her good friend. He'd come to her rescue many times. If it weren't for him, she'd be dead. She owed him her loyalty; however, she was torn. If she refuses to report what she knows, she could possibly endanger more lives. *"He seems to be guilty. I mean, everything seems to point toward him. Why does he keep popping up on crime scenes? Now I find the knife, rope, and condoms in his car, along with a pair of ladies' underwear."* She didn't know what to do next. She sat on the information for the time being.

Blaine finally woke. He noticed Jessica sitting on the sofa, looking confused. "Morning, Jessie," he said, walking to the bathroom. She stared at him suspiciously as he walked past her. *"How could he be so calm after all that's happened?"* She desperately wanted to bring up the subject but didn't know where to begin. If this were anyone else, she would've easily handed their ass to them on a platter, but this wasn't just anyone else. Instead of directly asking him any questions, she devised a plan to ease her way into the conversation. She asked him to take her to get breakfast. She hoped to start a discussion about the items and have him explain why he had them. As soon as he came out of the bathroom, she engaged in a little small talk with him. "Hey Blaine, I'm sort of hungry. Let's run out for some breakfast. Since I'm low on gas, let's take your car.

"Sure Jessie, let me get dressed."

After arriving at the restaurant, he parked the vehicle. Jessica got out and said, "Blaine, I think my cell phone fell between the seats." She said this so he'd have no choice but to explain the items in the back. They both got out, and he helped her look for her phone. She watched as he looked at the evidence. He looked at her, and she pretended not to notice. She then said, "Here it is. It was in my pocket the entire time." He didn't mention the evidence, but she decided not to say anything just yet. She wanted to watch him for a while. They both went to the restaurant. After a few minutes, Blaine excused himself and went out to his car. He carefully placed all the evidence in the trunk of his car and quickly walked back into the restaurant. Jessica had been watching him but pretended she hadn't.

For the next two weeks, she placed him under surveillance, watching him day and night. Around two in the morning, he would leave his home and ride around town frequented by local prostitutes. Then, he would go home and sleep in for a few hours. Sometimes, he would spend time with his children, and afterward, he would be roaming the streets of the city again

One night, she watched as he was out on the stroll. He was on Wright Avenue. She used her binoculars to watch as he pulled alongside a couple of women walking. He appeared to be talking to the ladies. He was slowly cruising alongside them as they were walking. Jessica watched as his vehicle came to a complete stop, and he got out. The other two ladies continued walking while Blaine and one of the women talked. Blaine stood close to her, leaning against his vehicle with his arms crossed as he spoke with her. After a few minutes of chatting, he went around to the passenger side of his vehicle and opened the door for her. She got in, and he quickly pulled away from the curb. Jessica followed behind them for fifteen minutes. He pulled into a convenience store's parking lot on University Avenue, and the girl went inside while he was in the car. She returned to the car, and they proceeded to Blaine's home.

Jessica called Blaine from her cell phone while watching him from a distance. She got no answer. She was disturbed by his behavior. She didn't want to just sit there in case the girl was in danger, but she felt the need to stand by and watch. She wanted to trust him but was also alarmed by his recent activities and strange behavior. She leaned back in her seat and watched the house. If he were to hurt the girl, she was sure he wouldn't do it in his own home. Before realizing it, she had fallen asleep, and when she opened her eyes, she panicked. Blaine had left before sunrise. She frantically reached for her cell phone and called him.

He answered immediately. "Blaine, where are you?"

"Good morning to you too, ma'am!"

"Good morning, Blaine." Blaine let out a chuckle.

"What's up Jessie?"

"Nothing much. What are you doing?"

"I'm getting breakfast, and I'm headed back home; why, do you need something?

"Is it okay for me to meet you at your place?"

"Sure, I'll be home in about fifteen minutes; if not, let yourself in."

"Okay, see you there." She ended the call and immediately pulled up to his home, got the key, and went inside. She looked around for signs of violence. She found nothing. She went through his drawers thoroughly while listening for him. She went into the garage and looked around. Knowing he could show up at any minute, she began looking through his toolboxes. She looked in a small locker that was filled with junk. When searching through the locker, she saw a duffel bag. In it, she found the rope, the box of condoms, the knife, and the underwear that she noticed from the backseat of Blaine's car. She took her phone out, took a picture, and put the things back as she found them. She heard the whirring sound from the garage door opening. Blaine was about to pull in. She hurried inside and took a seat. Blaine came inside and dropped the food on the table. He took a paper plate out of the cabinet and looked at Jessica.

"I hope you haven't eaten already. I got you something just in case." He handed her a breakfast sandwich. She took it and sat back.

"So, what brings you by so early?"

"Nothing really. I was out working on your case following new leads."

"So, what have you come up with?"

"You know Blaine, I'm not sure yet. I'll let you know when I get something concrete. So, what have you been up to lately?

"I've been laying low for a while. I think I'm going to go back to work. I'm going crazy just sitting around the house. I tried working from home but that's getting old."

Jessica began thinking about their years of friendship, wondering if she may have been wrong about him all along. If he were a killer, she should've seen the signs along the way. The Blaine Cooper she knew was an outstanding officer and a great man. He was practically like a brother to her. Then she thought of the time he saved her life. She felt she would be betraying him if she turned him in. But she found it difficult to ignore the evidence before her. But being a former police officer, he would've known to cover his tracks better than what he was doing, especially since evidence of the crimes was all over his home. She wondered why he picked up the prostitute. Where was she? Was she safe? Did he drop her off somewhere or did he kill her? Her mind raced as Blaine continued to speak. She noticed him waving his hand in front of her face. Trying to make eye contact he asked,

"Jessica, what's wrong? You've hardly touched your breakfast." She looked at him with a faint smile and said, "I'm sorry. I was just thinking about something. So, what did you do last night?" The question had been on the tip of her tongue the entire time. She was thinking about it so deeply that she wondered if she actually asked. He answered.

"I couldn't rest so I went riding. After a while, I came back home."

"Were you alone?" As she anxiously waited for the answer to her question, his cell phone rang. He quickly answered.

"Hello. Well good morning to you too. You're very welcome," She overheard him say to the caller. He got up from the table and walked into the other room for more privacy. She could hear his conversation faintly. She could only hear his side of the conversation. "No problem. Anytime you need me, just give me a call okay. I'm here to help in any way I can. Remember what I said. Be careful out there. Okay, goodbye."

He ended his call and went back into the kitchen where Jessica was still sitting. He didn't say who he had been talking to. She only hoped it was the young lady he picked up.

"Friend of yours?"

"Yeah, she found herself in a jam, so I wanted to help her out." He quickly changed the subject. She wanted to pry but she decided against it for now. She continued to keep her eyes on him.

CHAPTER FIVE

The young lady that Blaine stopped to help on the side of the road was getting better. Her name was Felicia Sims. It had been a couple of weeks since the attack. An officer had been stationed outside her room for her protection. She was on an extended stay in the hospital for severe complications due to her injuries. She held the clue to who her would-be killer was. She faced a killer and was able to live to tell about it. The only difference in her case is that she was stabbed possibly for fighting back. The other women were all strangled, some with broken necks. The police wanted to know what happened that caused the killer to forgo his normal plan. Detective Armstrong was there to question her. There was also a female detective there. She was holding her hand for support. She was shown a picture of Blaine to see if she could remember him. Reaching for the photo she looked at the picture and turned her head to the side.

"Ma'am, do you recognize this man?" She shook her head and closed her eyes. She refused to answer any more questions. All they could do was wait and go off the evidence they had. They decided to call Blaine back in for more questioning. He willingly went to the police station. He was taken to the interrogation room and Detective Armstrong began speaking.

"Blaine as you know we have you down here to speak with you about what happened a couple of weeks ago. Now the young lady, Ms. Sims, is cooperating with the police. We want to get your side of the story. Can you please tell me again what happened that night?"

"I know you're doing your job, but if you're going to keep calling me down here every time y'all find a body or a woman gets hurt, I'm wondering why I was even allowed to make bond."

"With all due respect Blaine, you were caught with two of the women in question."

"That may be so, but you know I didn't hurt either of those women. Ask her, and she'll tell you. I was only there to help."

"Explain to me what happened again."

"It was around nine-thirty; I had just left from dropping off my boys. As I proceeded to my home, about a block and a half away from my ex-wife's place, I noticed her car

122

in the middle of the road. I got out of my vehicle and walked over to her. I saw she was in distress, so I opened the door to help her. She fell out of the car and into my arms. I helped her as much as I could and then called for help. If I wasn't there to help her, why would I call the police? If I wanted to harm her, I would've done that and gone on about my business. I don't know her, and I've never met her before. If I hadn't gotten help for her, I'm sure she would be dead by now. I would never hurt anyone least of all women and children. I know I'm guilty of beating that child predator's ass, but that's about as violent as I've ever gotten with anyone. The thought of someone so vile like that harming children, pissed me off. While I was arresting him, he asked me if I had young boys. I refused to answer. He then proceeded to tell me in detail how he would harm them. He whispered such vulgarities to me about my boys and I lost it. So yeah, I beat his ass. If the other officers hadn't pulled me off him, I probably could've hurt him far worse than I did. I let him get to me. If we hadn't caught him, he would still be out there harming children. I know I cost the department a lot of money, but he deserved that ass-whipping, and I enjoyed giving it to him. Don't act as if you've never roughed up a suspect before. I know as police officers; we're not above the law. I should've left it up to the justice system but when he threatened my boys, I snapped. Getting into a scuffle with a suspect is one thing, but hurting innocent people just isn't my thing."

"Blaine, I'm sorry but I have a job to do. I'm not trying to make accusations against you, I just want to get to the bottom of this and get this case solved."

"Well, I'm not the one running. I'm here and I've always been here. I've made myself available to law enforcement. Now let me ask you this; while you're busy focusing on me, where's the couple that worked at the bar? You know, the ones who drugged me. What have you done to find them? I'm not the key to solving this case, perhaps they are. If you would put a little more time and effort into trying to find them, maybe you'll solve your cases. Now if you don't need anything else from me, may I leave?"

"Yes; you may go for now, but I don't need to tell you not to leave town."

With a look of disgust, Blaine said, "Thanks for your confidence in me my friend, and to think, I was in your wedding." Detective Armstrong looked at him and exhaled. Blaine walked out. He was heartbroken. It appeared as if some of his friends were turning on him and they seemed to believe he was guilty. He left the station and went and sat in a nearby park. He watched the families laughing and playing with their children. He longed for the innocent days of his past; the days when he could walk around without a cloud of suspicion hanging over him. He leaned back on the bench and looked up at the clear blue sky. He said a brief prayer and left.

Back at the Barnes detective agency, Jessica was sitting at her desk. Her mother was on her computer typing away at the keys. The sound of the keystrokes faded in the background as Jessica began to think about Blaine. She was contemplating confronting him on the issues of the evidence. She knew she was morally obligated to turn over any information she found. Because of him, she's alive. He'd done many wonderful works in the community. If she was wrong and he's not the killer, it could cost her their friendship and the close bond they've come to share over the many years. After thinking about the subject, she decided she would go ahead and confront him. She sat up in her chair. Her mother's back was to her, but she could hear Jessica shifting around. "Jessica honey, do you have something on your mind? You've been very quiet over there. What are you thinking about?"

"Nothing really Mom, I have a few things I need to take care of that's it."

"Is there something I can do for you?"

"No, it's personal." Jessica looked as if she wanted to ask her a question. Without thinking, she said, "Mom I want to run a scenario by you, and I want your honest opinion okay." Her mother turned away from the computer screen and gave her full attention to her daughter.

"What is it dear?"

"If you have proof that a family member of yours has possibly committed a heinous crime, how likely are you to turn them in? Let's say if it were me. Would you turn me in?"

Her mother exhaled and asked, "Did you find something on Blaine dear?" Jessica looked at her mother almost like a deer who'd gazed into the headlights of oncoming traffic. Trying to hide why she was asking the question, she quickly looked away. She didn't answer her.

Her mom was very wise and thus she began to offer her advice.

"You know what I think. The people of our past are not the people of our future. Just because we think we know someone doesn't mean we can truly know *everything* about them. I know your friend saved your life. I know you love him but there's no way of knowing what a person is truly capable of. People are sick these days. They can live seemingly functional lives carrying on in the community fooling others into thinking they're perfectly normal. Some people are killers; it's just as simple as that. They reason in their minds that killing is okay by dehumanizing their intended victims. Some kill, thinking society would be a better place without certain types of individuals in this case prostitutes, perhaps child molesters or child abusers. Others kill simply for the thrill and the sport of it. To continue their hunting, they must blend in and function well with others.

Some killers are sadistic and egotistical, and they want to brag about what they've done by leaving a calling card or a message. If the police pin their crimes on someone else, they get angry and continue to kill to prove their worth and value. It's sort of an art with them if you will. They possess the skill and ability to kill precisely while staying a few steps ahead of society. The killer uses this world as his hunting ground. A skillful hunter wants to sneak up on his prey. To do so, he must blend into his surroundings, so he camouflages himself by masking his true identity and motives thereby fooling everyone in his circle. There was once a study that asked women what qualities they would want in an ideal mate. Funny thing is, the characteristics they required most in a mate fit the description of most serial killers. Yes, we know and love Blaine, but think of all the people society was wrong about. I mean, how well do you really know people? No one can truly vouch for anyone because you just can't know everything there is about a person. There are so many coincidences in this case and Blaine has been caught with the dead body of a woman in his car. Then you said he was found with another young lady who had been stabbed in her car. It's enough to make you wonder. I really don't want to believe he has done this, but with evidence like that, it's pretty compelling. To tell you the truth, I'm surprised he's still out on bail. It shocked me that the judge even granted bail in the first place given the extreme nature of the crime.

In my opinion, if you know something, you should report it. You don't want others getting hurt due to your silence. Yes, Blaine may have saved your life but that doesn't mean others have to die because of it. You'll be just as guilty if you keep your silence and he's the killer."

Jessica knew there was no use in lying to her and trying to pretend she wasn't talking about Blaine. Her mother always had the keenest of instincts. That's where she got her detective gene from. That's why they work so well together at the detective agency. Through the many years whenever a case would stump her, she would sit back and regroup. She would talk to her mother who would always help her to see things in a much clearer light. She knew her mother was right about reporting what she knew. Her mother didn't say anything else. She looked at Jessica with a warm motherly smile. Jessica was comforted. She looked at her mother's beautiful face; she loved how her eyes sparkled and the youthfulness of her facial features that made her appear far younger than her age. She was in her mid-sixties and not a wrinkle in sight. The only thing remotely showing her age is her choice not to dye her salt and pepper hair which she kept cut in a short pixie style. She turned around and began typing on her computer again. Jessica tried to finish working on her cases, but she couldn't concentrate on what she was doing. Blaine was still on her mind.

Jessica had no siblings. The closest person she has to a brother is Blaine. Spending many years together as partners and his saving her life brought them even closer. She loved him but not only that, she felt indebted to him for what he had done for her. Blaine was thoughtful and very kind. The mere thought of hurting him weakened her and although she's hard as nails it almost brought her to tears. She had been allowing Blaine's case to take its toll on her. She wasn't getting much rest because she was tailing him through the night and working throughout the day. She was a bit emotional because she wanted to believe in him. She followed Blaine continually hoping he would lead her to what he was really into. Some nights he would give girls money and on others, he would sit and talk to them. She wanted so badly for him to be innocent but there were times that his guilt seemed to be evident, especially with all the things she'd learned from watching him. It was time to confront him with the evidence and go to the police with what she had. Her life was about to change as she knew it, but she had to do the right thing.

CHAPTER SIX

It was six in the evening and Blaine went to Cindy's club. He walked in and looked around for her. He spotted her clearing a table and speaking with a couple of ladies. She looked up at him and smiled. Hoping the visit was a personal one, she was delighted to see him. She walked over to where he was standing. "Blaine my friend, how have you been?" She gave him a lingering hug. He kissed her on the cheek.

"I'm hanging in there Cindy, how are you?"

She looked around the club and said, "As you can see, we're getting ready for another busy night. Have you had dinner yet?"

"I had a light lunch. It was nothing special. Do you think you can get your chef to fix me a little something?"

"I sure can sugar. What will you have?"

"Tell him I'd like a large bone-in rib eye, medium-well with a loaded baked potato, lots of sour cream, and a large iced tea, and a slice of that cheesecake with chocolate sauce."

"Damn sugar. I see you're living a little dangerously with that diet. You're usually so health conscious. Are you sure you want to eat all of that?" By the expression on his face, she knew he meant it.

"Well sugar, I'll be right back." She put in his order and went back to sit with him.

"So, what brings you by?" she asked, admiring him as she has done for many years.

"I'm here to ask you a few questions about the young lady that was working here at the club. You know the girl that tried to drug Jessica's drink. What can you tell me about her?"

"You know, I'm a friend to most of the girls. She came to me seeking a job. She said she was new in town, and she wanted to work her way through school, so I gave her a job. She was a hard worker for the little time she was here. She seemed motivated and eager to work. She didn't talk much about her life. She was a beautiful girl even though she chose the Gothic look, but it worked for her. She had her share of fans here and made plenty of tips. She could mix a mean drink too. I was surprised when Jessica and Armstrong discovered what she'd done. About an hour before they came in to look at the video, she left in hurry and I haven't seen her since. The police asked me a million questions about her, and I gave them everything I had and told them all I knew. I run a legitimate establishment, and I'd like to keep it that way. I lived my life on the streets for many years. It was great to get clean, so I don't have to look over my shoulder from those johns on the street to the police or would-be gangsters. I don't want any trouble. She passed the drug screen, so I let her work. Normally we do a background check on them but I'm a sucker for a sad story, so I helped her. Things seemed to work out until that incident with Jessica."

"So, you haven't seen her since that day?"

"No, I haven't." He looked around as if he was disappointed to hear what she was telling him.

"So, what have you been up to lately Blaine?"

"I've been spending as much time with my children as I can. Life's too precious to waste." Cindy reached for Blaine's hand.

"If it's any consolation sugar, you know I don't believe for one minute that you hurt any of those girls. I know you're innocent."

Their eyes locked. He squeezed her hand. "Cindy, you don't know how much it means for me to hear you say that. It seems that everyone around me is starting to doubt my innocence. Only you and Jessie seem to be in my corner."

"Blaine, I never really thanked you for the many times you helped me when I was out there. You were so good to me. I thank you for all the kind words and your pep talks; they never fell on deaf ears. You may have thought I wasn't listening to you, but I heard every positive word you ever spoke into my life and I took them in. I know I was tough back then, and I got into a lot of trouble. It was rough out there on those streets. You seemed to be one of the few officers who wanted to help us girls instead of always running us downtown."

He smiled and said, "You're one tough lady but I knew you were doing what you felt you had to in order to survive. I knew you wouldn't be out there long. You seemed to get it. You motivated the other girls to do better. You had a great heart, even when you were at your lowest. I never gave up on you. I knew you could do it. Now, look at you. You're clean and have a thriving business. I know some people still judge you for your past but not me."

"It's always been my dream to open my own restaurant. I knew I wanted to own a nightclub as well. As you know, I was an exotic dancer among other things. I wanted to mix that with a burlesque style of dance, all in a sexy, laid-back atmosphere with great food, music, and wonderful drinks. It's an event that couples can enjoy together and as you can tell by my patrons, they do. Our shows sell out every night. Do you know multi-million-dollar deals are made right here in this place? I've seen everyone from politicians to millionaires all here in *my* place enjoying themselves. I love this place. It's my life, my bread, and butter. It's a dream come true."

While she was talking, a beautiful waitress brought his food to the table. Blaine tore into the food, eating like a hungry animal hardly allowing himself to swallow before taking the next bite.

"Damn, Blaine. Slow down. What's the rush? You're not even tasting your food."

"Girl, do you know how long it's been since I had one of these steaks?"

"Slow down and enjoy it. Besides, I kinda like the company. Would you like to stay for the show? It starts around seven-thirty." Looking unconvinced he said,

"No Cindy, I just came by to talk to you about that young lady who worked here." She asked him flirtingly,

"What do you have to do tonight? I would love for you to stay and be my special guest. I'll have a treat for you." She gently rubbed the back of his hand in a seducing manner while gazing into his eyes.

"I guess I can stay. What do you have for me? I'm curious."

"You're just going to have to wait and see," she said while continuing to look at him seductively.

"Hmm.. I think I like the sound of that," he said smiling. Cindy was very beautiful and although she spent years in a cruel harsh world, the effects of what she'd gone through, never showed on her face or her body.

"That meal is on the house you know. I'm headed to the bar to get you a drink. What would you like?"

"Hennessy"

"Okay, I'll be right back."

Blaine decided to stay a while, so he settled in. He had nothing else to do and he was quite fond of Cindy. He watched her as she handled her business, telling each young lady what to do. He thought of the days when she was on the streets. There was always something special about her. She was rough around the edges, but she was always a good girl. She never bothered anyone, and her only crimes were fighting to protect the girls on the street and prostitution. She used drugs for a brief span after the death of her son. If one didn't know her before, they would've never known the many hardships she suffered. She looks every bit of the increasingly powerful businesswoman that she was. Blaine watched as Cindy began walking toward him with his drink. He stared at her as her hips swayed and her thighs moved. Her breast jiggled as she quickly approached the table. In an almost hypnotic state, his eyes were still focused on her body. He hardly noticed that she had set his drink on the table.

"Here you are sugar."

Still watching her he said, "Have a seat for a minute."

"I can't right now, the shows are about to start. Come over to the stage I have a special seat for you in the VIP section."

He smiled and said, "Wow, the VIP section, what did I do to deserve that?"

A hostess walked over to his table and gathered his food and drink and placed them on a serving tray. Cindy placed her hands on her hips and said, "Don't ask questions. Follow Lindsey and she'll take you to your seat." As he stood to his feet, she leaned in and whispered in his ear. "I hope you enjoy your evening." He felt the warmth of her breath. As she was speaking, her soft lips lightly touched his ear, and she proceeded to kiss him. He caught a whiff of her expensive perfume. His heart fluttered and as chills came over his body, his penis began to stiffen.

Blaine knew she was flirting with him. She always did a mild form of flirting in the past, but nothing like this. He continued watching her as he was being escorted to his seat. He was eager to know what she was up to. With a napkin in hand, he placed it over the bulge in his pants while being escorted to the VIP section. After being seated, the lights were dimmed. A sultry voice could be heard over the speakers. Multi-colored lights were shining on the stage as two beautiful, scantily clad young women came out. They danced to a perfectly choreographed dance as the sultry voice in the background recited a sensual erotic poem to the sounds of soothing music. A handsome young man bulging with muscles slowly walked on the stage and engaged in an erotic dance with each of the ladies as the poem dictated what was taking place. The show continued and several more routines were performed. After the last skit, two very beautiful black women stepped down from the stage walking over to Blaine. They took him by each arm and escorted him to the stage. He was nervous but he knew he couldn't turn back now. The patrons of the restaurant applauded as he was taken to the stage. The lights went low again, and he heard soft music playing as the two ladies danced on either side of him so he wouldn't be on stage alone. He heard Cindy's voice.

Lights were shining on her as she made her grand entrance on the stage. Dressed in a shimmering peach, long-flowing revealing gown, she slowly and seductively walked over to him. The two young ladies exited the stage, and the lights were solely on her as she gracefully danced around him lightly caressing his chest. In her most sensual voice, she began to recite her poetry. He looked at her breast. He could see her erect nipples through the sheer fabric. He began to salivate. She spoke to the rhythm of the music,

"When I close my eyes, I see you in my dreams. You've come to fill me with your love. When I sense your presence, we begin to dance to the rhythm of our song. The desired touch, a glance, a oneness. As I gaze into your eyes, my lips covet your kiss; a kiss that will surely awaken the passion inside. My body quickens as we embark upon a spiritual journey. For many years our love was my secret alone, hidden in my heart, longing to be free. Freedom is now. The time has come for us to release our love and let it soar on the wings of destiny.

She gently took him by both hands and placed them on her curvy hips. She slid up and down in a rhythmic motion rubbing her body against his while telling him all she wanted of him; spilling all her secrets of the many years she'd admired him. He was lost in her touch and captivated by her words. He took heed as he could tell the poem was tailor-made specifically for him. She continued the poem and the erotic dance with him. As her piece was ending, she placed his hand on her chest close to her heart. She stood staring into his eyes hoping he would catch on to the fact that she was not only performing, but she was pouring out her very soul. She leaned in to kiss him lightly on the lips. Her back was to the audience. She whispered, "You are *my dream,* Blaine."

He watched her as she moved in for another kiss, this time a little longer. As her lips lingered on his, the lights faded, and the crowd roared. The spotlights were turned back on them, and she stood by his side holding his hand as the audience gave a standing ovation. She bowed and pointed towards Blaine. He smiled nervously. She thanked him and walked backstage. The two young ladies came to escort him back to his seat. The show continued. Patrons were speaking to him and patting him on the back. It wasn't unusual for Cindy to bring guests on stage to participate in the shows. She does it very often because her audience enjoyed it. Although Blaine knew this, Cindy had piqued his interest. He could tell this was no ordinary skit. At least he hoped it wasn't. He decided he would remain at the club until closing. He waited for Cindy as everyone began exiting the club. After waiting for ten minutes, he saw her coming out with her briefcase and luggage which contained her make-up. A few employees were still in the building cleaning up. A large black security guard named Albert normally sees her in her vehicle each night. Standing at his post, he watched as she approached the exit.

"Ms. Cindy, allow me to get that for you," he said reaching for her small suitcase. Cindy noticed Blaine waiting for her.

"Thanks, Big Al, but I think I'll be alright." She walked closer to Blaine. She handed him her briefcase. Concerned for Cindy's safety, Big Al gave him a threatening look. Blaine noticed and silently communicated through facial expressions that she was safe and in good hands. As they were walking to the parking lot, Blaine said,

"Your show was great tonight,"

"Thank you, sugar. I hope you didn't mind me bringing you on stage in front of all those people."

"I didn't mind. I *was* a little nervous, but with you there it was okay." He wanted to ask her about the performance but said nothing. She was curious as to what he was thinking, so she asked,

"How did you like the poem?"

"I thought it was beautiful. I enjoyed it."

"Thank you." She went silent. They walked towards a white Mercedes S class. She pressed the remote unlocking the trunk. He placed the suitcase inside and then he walked to the driver's side of the vehicle. He opened the door for her and held it as she placed her purse inside.

"Cindy, I'm curious. What do you do when you leave here?"

"I love winding down with a glass of wine and some soothing music. I write my poetry and afterwards I go to sleep."

"So, there's no one special in your life?"

"Yes, but he doesn't know it." She slowly lifted her head. Their eyes met. She smiled at him.

"Why haven't you expressed your feeling towards him?"

"I couldn't. It's all a foolish dream, besides the timing was off." After a long pause, she said,

"Well, I guess I'll be heading home." She lightly tugged on her door. Blaine, looking as if he wanted to say something, wouldn't allow the door to close. She could sense it, so she asked,

"Would you like to come over for a cup of coffee? That is if you don't have anything else to do."

"Sure, I can do that. Are you sure it would be okay?"

"Yes, I'm sure. Follow me." She got in her car and closed the door. She waited on him while he went to get his vehicle. He pulled his vehicle behind hers and followed her to her home. They drove down Asher Avenue and turned right on Fair Park Blvd. They hit interstate six-thirty and headed west. Blaine had never visited her home. She lived in a gated community out close to the Wellington Heights subdivision. He could hardly believe how far she had come. She lived among doctors and lawyers and the elite business class people of the city of Little Rock, a far cry from the sleazy streets of the ghetto from which he used to rescue her. She went from seedy motel rooms to easy street, but it didn't come easy. She paid her dues to be where she was, and it was well deserved. She had truly come up for sure. She always had style and class ever since he could remember.

She finally made the left turn into her community. He pulled in behind her and waited while she waved her card over the sensor, and they waited for the large wrought iron gate as it slowly opened. He followed her for another five minutes as she drove up to her home. He was quite impressed. A white gentleman was standing in the driveway waiting to take her car. Blaine exited his vehicle and went up to her to assist in any way he could. He walked her inside.

"Damn Cindy, this is a beautiful home. Did you hit the lotto or something?"

"No sugar, it's all hard work. Sleepless nights and restless days but it's finally paid off for me. To tell you the truth, I enjoy it better knowing I worked my ass off to have these things." The gentleman walked in and placed her keys where they belonged. He went through the home and gathered his things.

"Cindy, do you need anything else this evening?"

"No Randy, I'm good. I thank you."

He walked to the door and said, "Well, I'll see you tomorrow." He left. She motioned for Blaine to have a seat. Impressed, he said,

"Go ahead, girl. I see you have your very own butler and everything."

She laughed, "Randy is not my butler, he's my cousin and he sees to it that I get in safe since I work late, and he does other minor things around the home for me. His wife helps me with the cleaning in the daytime. I don't like bringing just anyone into my home. I may hire someone to work at the club and even then, we run checks on them, but I don't trust anyone in my home but family."

Cindy went into the kitchen and started the coffee. She took a few snack cakes out and placed them on a small platter then walked back to where Blaine was sitting and placed them on the table in front of him. While the coffee was brewing, she went into her bedroom and took a quick shower. She came out looking even more beautiful. She had no make-up on, only a hint of lip gloss. Her hair was very long, down to her buttocks. She looked fresh and wholesome and untainted by the world. One would think she never touched drugs. She walked past Blaine, and he couldn't help but stare. He was intoxicated by the scent of her perfume. He thought, *"Damn Cindy is very beautiful."* She was wearing a pair of glamorous, black satin pajamas.

"Blaine, how do you like your coffee Hun?"

"It doesn't matter," he said. She brought in everything from multi-flavored creamers to sugars and sweeteners. She placed them next to the snacks and sat next to Blaine. She poured him a cup of coffee and he fixed it to his liking. She leaned back on the sofa.

"Cindy, look at this empire you've built. You're an amazing success story and the epitome of a successful woman. You have everything."

"I wouldn't say *everything*," she said looking at him seductively. "The only thing that's missing is that special guy who has always held the key to my heart."

"Who could that be?" he asked curiously. She lifted her coffee cup to her lips and sipped while playfully cutting her eyes at him. She placed the cup on the serving tray and pulled her feet up on the sofa. He leaned back in a reclining position.

"So, are you going to answer my question?" She looked at him and simply smiled. "I'm just curious. That piece you did tonight on stage; what inspired you to write that? Or should I ask who? Could it be the man you hope to attain one day?"

"Are you using your law enforcement instincts to get into my personal affairs?" He smiled looking into her beautiful hazel eyes. He wanted her to say more. He was trying to read her. The expression on her face and her refusal to give him a straight answer made him even more curious. He leaned in closer and gently touched her hand.

"Cindy, you're amazing." Her heart ached for him. She was almost brought to tears when he leaned in for a kiss. He was paying attention to her. She finally felt she was worthy of him, unlike their initial meeting years ago. Working as a patrol officer, he was newly married with no children. She was moved by his kindness and compassion. During his shift. he would counsel her and the other girls, teach them self-defense techniques, and often feed them or pay for a hotel so they could get off the streets for a night. He even went to court with them or just lent a helping hand whenever needed. Blaine went from being a young husband and rookie cop to a divorced father of two. While his life was changing, Cindy's life was changing too, hers for the better. She developed a crush on him, creating fantasies of him rescuing her from her dire street life. Realizing her dreams were unrealistic, she began to take control of her life and started building her dreams. She thought of him often. Now he's in her home, a moment she'd fanaticized about for years.

He kissed her and she melted in his arms. Her body trembled with excitement. She could feel the emotions in her release as he continued kissing her. She wanted to express her feelings for him with her body. She took him by the hand, and they walked into her bedroom kissing the entire time. He sat on her large bed and watched as she undressed, pulling the bottoms of her pajamas off. Not saying a word, she allowed her overthrow to fall from her shoulders revealing her perfectly nude body. Stunned by her goddess-like appearance, his heart began racing. He watched with anxious anticipation as she made her way over to him. She helped him out of his clothes. She loved his body in every way imaginable fulfilling all her desires. He was every bit the man she dreamed he would be. He loved her with much passion as he too needed her. With all he was facing, she was a welcome and therapeutic distraction. They made love through the night, two people desiring one another. Blaine was taken with her and he was turned on by her passion for him. He knew he was the dream in her poem. After making love, he held her close in his arms and for the first time, Cindy let her guard down and gave herself over to a man whom she felt deserved. No performance, no acting or pretense. There was no need to be harsh or hardcore with him. She expressed her softer, more feminine side. She was a lady, and he made her feel as such.

Overwhelmed with emotions, a tear fell from her cheek and landed on his chest. He looked down at her and lifted her chin. He kissed her tear-soaked face and then gently wiped them away with his thumb. He kissed her lips and said,

"I'm here." He held her tight as her emotions began to show. To lighten the mood, she laughed and said,

"So, you know my secret huh?"

"Yes, and I love it. Doesn't it feel so much better now that you've let me in on it?"

"Yes, it does. When did you know?"

"I've always known but now was the perfect time to act on it. Some boundaries were not to be crossed all those years ago and now that's no longer an issue. We are free to be whatever we want." They continued their newfound love language into the morning. Although Blaine was thrilled about what was taking place between, he and Cindy, he couldn't ignore the fact that there was a murder charge still looming.

CHAPTER SEVEN

Jessica made up her mind that she was going to turn over what she knew to the police, but she wanted to talk with Blaine first. She called him all morning but after getting no answer, she left several voice messages for him hoping he would return her calls soon. Not knowing he was with Cindy; she was afraid she'd lost track of him. She drove over to his place and noticed he wasn't there. She used the spare key to go inside. She went to the garage, to the place where she saw all the incriminating evidence and noticed it had been removed. She searched the house for it, but it was nowhere to be found. She put everything back where she found it and left.

In the meantime, Blaine was still at Cindy's enjoying her company. They were learning more about each other as lovers. They realized the possibility of their relationship could evolve into a more exclusive connection. Cindy was a loyal friend and a good person, so he wasn't in the least bit concerned about her former life. She was full of love and compassion, often going out of her way to help others. Blaine and Cindy spent the morning lounging. She was pleased when she opened her eyes, and he was still lying beside her. She smiled and snuggled close to him. He kissed her on the lips.

"Good morning beautiful."

"Good morning," she said with a warm smile. He held her closer.

"I enjoyed spending time with you," she said.

"I enjoyed you too. I don't want to leave."

"Trust me I don't want you to go."

"Let's just stay inside all day," he said.

"I would love to, but I have to open my business. You know how crazy that lunch crowd can be. If I'm not there, all hell would probably break loose. But we can spend another hour or two together. I could use a little pick-me-up. I'll call my staff and let them know I will be in later."

"Sounds like a great idea," he said.

She made her calls, and they spent a couple more hours together. They talked of Blaine's legal issues as well as his children. She poured her heart out to him, and he did the same.

"Cindy, I don't know what took us so long to make the connection, but you are heaven-sent. I mean you and I; it just makes sense. How could you hold your feelings for me so long?"

Cindy moved in closer and said, "I think people care about others more than they know but the reality of them getting together may not be what's best. You were married and I respected that. Back then, I felt we were from different worlds and there was no chance of us making a romantic connection. After your divorce, I noticed you were making transitions which seemed to be taking a toll on you so I didn't want to pursue you at that moment. I kept my feelings to myself knowing perhaps there was no chance of us ever getting together and I understood that. But seeing you last night, those old feelings which I thought were gone, had come back and they were stronger than ever. I couldn't deny my feelings for you. I didn't think much would come of it but I was feeling hopeful, so I took a chance and recited my poem. I never thought you would catch on. I pretended it was just another performance."

"I got it immediately. I sensed your essence. I was feeling the vibes. When you kissed me, electric energy flowed through my body and charged my heart. I felt like a new man. I'm grateful to you for opening that door, and my eyes. I knew you as Cindy, the girl from around the way but I want to get to know your heart. I can't tell you what the future may hold for us, but I definitely would love to keep seeing you; that is if you don't have a problem with it."

"No problem here sugar."

She was delighted to hear him express his feelings so openly and honestly.

They talked a little more and she got dressed and went to her place of business. Blaine went home. He was feeling great. He needed this connection. He felt the world was against him and being with Cindy made him forget all his troubles which seemed to fade as she soothed him and loved his body. After his divorce, he threw himself into his work at his consulting firm. He helped to co-parent his sons and he taught his self-defense classes as well as worked with Jessica at the agency. He never allowed the time for a romantic relationship. He smiled as he thought of Cindy. He could still smell her perfume on his clothes. The thought of seeing her again thrilled his heart. He drove home and showered and called his attorney. He checked his voice messages. *"Damn Jessica has left four messages. I wonder what could be so important,"* he said dialing her number. She picked up.

"Jessica, I have four messages from you, what's up."

"Blaine, I need to speak with you. It's important. I've been trying to reach you all night. Where have you been?"

"I've been with a friend, why?"

"Blaine I'm worried about you. May I come over now?"

"Yes, please hurry because I have a meeting with my attorney in a couple of hours so come on over."

Jessica dropped what she was doing and went to his place. Erring on the side of caution, she called her mother and told her where she would be. The door was open, so she let herself in where she found Blaine hurriedly gathering items. He had a large black duffel bag in his hand. He set it down on the floor next to him as he took a seat. Keeping her eye on the bag, Jessica took a seat too.

"What's so important Jessie that you had to see me?" She was nervous. She was having feelings of regret, but she felt she was doing the right thing.

"Blaine, I came by to speak with you. We've been friends for many years now. You're like a brother to me and I love you more than you know. I don't want you to get upset with me, but I need to ask; did you have anything to do with the murders of those women?" Blaine looked at her with disgust and disbelief.

"Are you serious Jessica? Don't tell me you believe I'm the Scorned killer too. I don't believe this." He stood to his feet and began nervously walking around. Jessica kept her eye on the duffel bag. "My own friend thinks I'm a murderer. So, tell me, have you been investigating me too?"

"Blaine, you know I have to look at every aspect of the case so yes that means investigating you too."

"So, tell me, good friend, what have you come up with so far?" She was a little hesitant to tell him, but he insisted.

"Blaine, I saw the knife, condoms, and the rope in your back seat. When we went for breakfast, you walked to the car and removed them. I saw them along with underwear in your garage. I came over here today and they were gone."

"So that makes me a killer, right?"

"Where's the missing evidence, Blaine?"

He leaned over and gave her the duffel bag. He threw it at her, and it landed at her feet.

"It's right here along with other evidence that you have yet to see." She opened the bag and just as he said, it was all there.

"I was on my way to my attorney's office to give it to her for her to turn it over to the police. These things just keep showing up at random. She's going to take them to the police and we're going to come up with a strategy to see who is doing this. It's supposed to be an undercover thing. I have a security company coming to install surveillance cameras because it seems someone has been getting into my home and car without my knowledge."

"But I've been following you around town in the middle of the night. Why do you leave like that? I saw you bring a young lady back here. What happened to her?"

"Wow, Jessica; Really? Well, since you must know, she was in trouble and needed a place to crash for the night. I let her stay here. I speak to women warning them to be careful. I'm concerned about them and it's hard sleeping at night knowing someone is out there killing them. I happen to know a couple of the young ladies that were killed. I don't want to see that happen to anyone else. These women are human beings not fair game for some sick killer.

Do you know how many of them have gotten their lives together and come off the streets to go on to live productive lives? The killer is taking that chance away from them. Some of them have children and although they're on the streets, they have families that truly love and care about them. Hell, I care about them! I can't believe you right now Jessica." He walked away and looked out of the window. With his hands on his hips, he looked back at Jessica in frustration. She knew he was upset with her, but she had to know the truth.

"Blaine, I'm sorry. I didn't mean to accuse you. Some of the evidence pointed to you and there were instances where you were acting very suspiciously."

"Jessie, I let you into my home. I trusted you. You have a key to my place. You always have access to me. I would be a fool to do this."

"Why didn't you come to me for help Blaine? I would have helped you."

"I didn't come to you because I was investigating this case myself. I needed legal help, so I called Karen Reed. Armstrong believes I'm guilty and so do you. I thought you were helping my case, but it seems you two have been working against me the entire time. I guess a man finds out who his friends are when he's down."

"Blaine that's not fair. Please try to see things from my point of view."

"Jessica, I don't have time to talk about this I have to leave, Karen is waiting on me."

Blaine got the duffel bag and left. Jessica sat on the sofa thinking. She called Blaine's attorney who confirmed the meeting. She decided to trust him for the time being. She didn't go to Detective Armstrong or the police just yet. Blaine seemed to be forthcoming.

Blaine took the evidence to his attorney and turned it over to her. After leaving her office, he called Cindy. They made plans to spend time together. He looked forward to seeing her again. She was the missing link in his chain. She managed to make him feel whole in the brief moment they were together. With her by his side and his children, he began looking forward to his future. He was energetic and more determined than ever to clear his name.

He called his ex-wife to make plans to pick up his children. She answered the phone.

"Sheila."

"Hello, Blaine."

"I want to see the children today."

"Blaine, I'm sorry but we're on our way to Louisiana. I've been trying to call you to let you know, but I couldn't get an answer. I called you all last night and this morning."

"Why didn't you leave me a message?"

"I thought you would call me back. Besides, you knew I was going to Louisiana. We'll be there until your legal issues are resolved. Virgil and I thought it would be the right time for me to leave. He's staying over because he has to work. We should be gone for a few weeks. You can speak to them daily."

"Sheila, you're breaking my heart. You know you shouldn't have left without giving me a chance to say goodbye. As a stipulation of my bond, I can't leave town which keeps me from visiting them."

"I'm sorry Blaine but you know it's not always about you. This is about your children. Think about them. Let me protect them from this media buzz and nosy people talking about it. Some of them are asking me questions in front of the children. We can't seem to get away from this no matter how hard we try. Trust me, it's for the best."

Blaine hesitated; he held the phone for a second. "Will you let me speak to them please?" Sheila handed the boys the phone and both boys took turns talking to their father. They expressed their excitement to Blaine about their trip. He was happy to hear their voices. After he and Sheila spoke a little more, they ended their call. He was upset to hear the news, but he realized there was little he could do. Jessica called him but when he saw it was her, he let it go to voicemail. He wasn't in the mood to talk to her. He went home hoping to be left alone but she was in the driveway waiting for him. He took a deep breath and exhaled. *She just won't give up. I wonder what she wants now.* " He pulled next to her vehicle and let down his window.

"What do you want Jessie? Are you here to accuse me again?"

"No Blaine. I came by to tell you we found Erin. You know the girl who worked at the bar. Two Baton Rouge police officers found her. Armstrong is taking her to the station now. She was in Baton Rouge holed up in a motel room. They can't find Arthur. We believe he saw the police and got spooked, but they're still searching. In the meantime, they'll hold Erin for tampering with the drinks. I don't know what they'll be discussing with her, but I thought I'd let you know that she was here in town."

Blaine was excited to hear the news. He parked his car and he and Jessica went inside. She talked with him while apologizing to him.

"Jessie, I know you love me, but I can't help but feel somewhat betrayed because you didn't trust me. You of all people should know I could never hurt anyone. Unless you actually saw me committing a crime, you should've given me the benefit of the doubt, but looking at things from your perspective, I guess I can understand. You hurt me though."

"I didn't mean to Blaine. I was simply trying to get at the truth, that's all any of us ever wanted."

"I understand, but you're still not off the hook."

"I know," she smiled. Wanting to make amends she asked,

"What are you eating for dinner this evening? Wanna go grab a bite?"

"No, not tonight. I have a date with a special lady." Jessica looked at him and said, "A date, since when?"

"Since yesterday."

"How is it you're seeing someone, and I know nothing about it?"

"Un-huh, see; while you were snooping around, you missed something right under your nose. You can't catch everything."

"Oh, you're going to tell me who this person is." He smiled and walked away.

"Blaine, you better tell me. Who is she?"

"I tell you what; why don't you use your detecting skills to see if you can find out."

"Oh, that is *so* not fair Blaine." They both laughed.

"I can tell you this. She's a friend of ours. She's a special young lady and I completely overlooked her as a potential catch but seeing her last night, Jessie, we made an instant connection. We've known each other for years.

She's a great woman. She has her shit together. She's amazingly beautiful and it turns out that she happens to have a certain admiration for yours truly. After spending quality time with her last night, it just fit. So, we're seeing each other again tonight." Blaine's smile was bright and beaming. He sounded giddy just speaking of Cindy. Jessica could tell whoever this lady was; she'd made quite an impact on her friend.

"She must be a special lady because I haven't seen a smile like that on your face in a while."

"I tell you, Jessie, outside of my kids, she is my ray of sunshine. She had me feeling as if I could conquer the world."

"Wow, she sounds amazing."

"Oh, she is. Cindy is one amazing woman." Jessica looked at him with her mouth hung open.

"Did you say, Cindy?"

"Yes, I said Cindy"

"You mean our Cindy Brooks from the Soiree over on Asher?"

"Yes, our Cindy"

"Oh my god! I can't believe it. But you know what, it fits strangely. I can almost see it. I mean Cindy *is* a good girl although she comes from a different background, she's changed from the woman we once knew back in the day. She's an established businesswoman, very sweet and kind-hearted too. Oh yeah, I can see that now. You know she's always been fond of you. So how does she feel about it?"

"She's the one who initiated it. I went by her business yesterday and things just sorta happened. It was fate." Blaine told her a little more without giving her any intimate details. She was happy for him. More so she was happy for Cindy. "Blaine I'm going to go home. I *done* heard it all today. I'm going to keep checking in with Armstrong to see if he can give us an update on Erin. Enjoy your evening. Tell Cindy I said hello."

Jessica left. Blaine hadn't really slept the night before since spending the night with Cindy, so he decided to take a nap. He was startled when his doorbell rang. He looked outside and noticed it was already dark. He'd slept longer than he had anticipated. He looked at the clock and noticed it was twenty minutes after eight. The doorbell rang again. He noticed it was Virgil. He opened the door for him.

"Hi, Blaine. I just wanted to stop by for a few minutes to chat with you." Blaine was a bit annoyed by the visit, but he allowed him to come inside.

"Have a seat." They sat at the dining room table. "Can I get you something to drink?"

"No, I'm okay. I came by to speak with you about the kids." Blaine walked to the refrigerator and got a bottle of water. Confused, he turned around and looked at Virgil.

"What about *my* children?"

"I want you to know that our decision to have Sheila take the children to Baton Rouge, is strictly in their best interest. It was nothing personal against you or your parenting abilities. It's your legal troubles that are haunting them. I know they may be your children, but Sheila is my fiancée, and I feel it's my responsibility to protect her and her children at all costs, even if it's from their father's demons."

"My demons? I guess coming from you that is supposed to mean I'm guilty of the crimes I'm accused of. It seems you have convinced Sheila to ship my children off. I didn't even get a chance to see them before they left. Virgil, I've never tried to interfere with what you and my

168

ex-wife have going on, but you will not dictate to me what will happen with my children. I know you're marrying their mother, and I can appreciate what you are trying to do with them, but I'm still their father and I still have joint custody of them regardless of my legal troubles." Blaine was getting heated. Virgil exhaled and said,

"I didn't want you to have to hear this from me, but we will be petitioning the court to have the joint custody removed until all this blows over. I'm hoping that you love your children enough not to fight this. You can see what this murder case is doing to them. Sheila is forced to have to explain to teachers, family members, and others about your murder charges. I mean how can a child live down the fact that their father is possibly a serial killer? I'm asking you to sign the forms when they come and not fight us on this." With rage brewing inside, Blaine stood to his feet. Trying to remain calm he said,

"I'm going to have to ask you to leave my home now." Virgil insisted on trying to make his point clear. Blaine got agitated.

"Get the fuck outta my house, now!" Virgil held his hands up in a surrendering motion and said,

"Okay, I'm leaving." He left. Blaine watched him as he backed out of the driveway. He called Sheila. When she answered, he told her everything that was discussed. Seeing he was upset, she calmed him.

"Blaine, I don't know what you're talking about. I don't have any plans of doing any of the things you suggested. I came to Louisiana temporarily. I have no intention of filing any papers in any court to remove joint custody. That would devastate the boys. We're here to visit Mom and to wait until your name is cleared. I would never agree to something like that. Are you sure Virgil suggested it because I know I didn't?" Blaine began to think for a minute. What was going on? Virgil spoke as if he and Sheila had agreed on the idea. He couldn't believe what she was saying.

"Sheila, he was sitting in my dining room less than five minutes ago. He said the both of you already agreed to it."

"Well, I don't know what's going on. We've never even discussed it. I'll call him. I wonder what possessed him to come by there. If I were to decide to take such drastic measures, I would definitely tell you myself. I wouldn't send my fiancé. These are our children, and I wouldn't take them from you even if you were convicted. I believe you're innocent, I just want to protect the children until you're cleared."

Hearing Sheila's take on the subject, Blaine calmed down a little but now he was angry with Virgil for the trouble he was causing. Sheila allowed him to talk to the kids and they ended their call. He proceeded with his night, meeting up with Cindy at the club and later going home with her and spending the rest of the night with her.

CHAPTER EIGHT

Detective Armstrong had been interviewing Erin. In the beginning, she was hard and cold, and she wouldn't tell him anything, but when it became clear that Arthur wasn't coming to her rescue, she grew tired and weary. She was also tired of running. Feeling trapped like a caged animal, she began to tell him everything she knew.

"Around six months ago, Arthur and I were called out of Baton Rouge by someone only known to us as *"The Boss,"* The boss said we were to watch Blaine Cooper and his best friend Jessica Barnes until we were told to act. We watched them at the detective agency and monitored their every move. We were told to get jobs at the pub downtown. That's where Blaine loved to go for drinks. I got a job at Cindy's Soirée on Asher because we were told they were always there.

Blaine loved the pub, but they both seemed to frequent the Soirée. I knew who Jessica was when she came into the club the day after Blaine Cooper was arrested. She was snooping around, trying to feel me out, so I tried to slip a little something into her drink, but she didn't take it. The night that Blaine was at the pub, Arthur and I were there. Arthur told me to drug his beers, so I did. I think I gave him too much. The boss had someone outside waiting for him. I think they were in a cab. Arthur drove Blaine's car while the other guy took him away from the pub. After that, I saw the guy on the news, and he'd been accused of killing that girl.

Blaine Cooper didn't kill those girls. We've been following him for a few months and every time the boss called, another girl died. I think Arthur helped to kill those women. I didn't see him do it, though. Arthur has changed. We used to pull a lot of jobs together, and they paid well for the most part, but this job paid so well that we settled here for six months. I love making money, but I didn't sign on for murder. After we went back to Baton Rouge, I continued to ask Arthur if he had anything to do with the murders. He confessed to me that while he didn't kill the girls, he helped to set up Blaine. They placed him in that car that night. They wanted him to be caught in that vehicle. That's all I know."

"So, you don't know why Blaine was targeted?" Detective Armstrong asked.

"I have no clue. It was crazy because he was such a nice guy. He was always helping others. He spent a lot of time with his children, too. Seemed like a regular guy."

She gave a videotaped confession of her role in the attempt to frame Blaine, and she also gave a sworn written statement. After giving them all the details, she gave them places she thought Arthur could be hiding. She was taken back to her holding cell, where she was able to sleep due to clearing her conscience. She was relieved. She just wanted to do her time and go on about her life. She was awakened by the guard telling her she had made bail. An anonymous attorney paid her bond.

Word immediately got back to Detective Armstrong. He found out who the attorney was and called him to ask who bonded her out and why. The attorney said he was contacted anonymously. Someone paid cash for his fees and asked that he act as her attorney and bond her out. He was forthcoming with the police. He informed the detective that while he was still signing the papers for her release, he looked around and saw that she was gone. They immediately went looking for her. In the meantime, Blaine's attorney, Karen Reed, made an appointment with the police to give them the evidence Blaine had given to her. She and Blaine met with detectives, telling them everything they learned from Erin. Charges were expected to be dropped against him, and although they had a signed and taped confession of Erin's account, they were desperately searching for her. She would be needed in court.

Jessica was informed about Erin's confession. She was excited for Blaine. Knowing that he was innocent was a relief to not only her but all who knew him. Somehow, the news media got wind of it and aired the facts of the case, and charges were expected to be dropped against Blaine. A spokesman for the police department confirmed the statements were true. They then called Karen Reed, his attorney, and she confirmed the news. They also aired they were looking for Erin Rogers and Arthur Manley. They posted pictures of them on all media outlets.

Blaine called Sheila and told her everything that was happening. He told her it would be for the best if she and the children stayed on over in Louisiana until they could find who it was that was purposely setting him up. He didn't know how far the person would go to harm him or his family. After ending the call with her and the kids, he called Cindy. She was excited to hear the news, and to celebrate, she suggested they spend the evening together. She made plans to take a little time away for her and Blaine. He was happy he could finally return to work and live his life in peace. He had a new lease on life. He was given a second chance and planned on hitting the ground running. He went home, shaved, and then hopped in the shower. He took out a nice, clean suit. After getting dressed, he called Cindy to let her know he was on his way. As he was ready to leave, he heard a familiar voice. Then, in an instant, he felt the cold steel barrel of a gun against the back of his neck.

"Don't move, or I will blow your fucking brains all over this garage. Now put your hands up and back towards me." Blaine did as he was told.

"Why are you doing this?" Blaine asked.

"Shut up!" With blunt force, Blaine was knocked over the back of the head and went unconscious.

It was getting late, and Cindy was still waiting for Blaine, who was a no-show. She went home to get ready for their date. When the set time they agreed upon had come and gone, Cindy called Blaine repeatedly. After not getting a response, she called Jessica. She was concerned after not hearing from him, and it was going on ten thirty at night.

"Jessica, I can't find Blaine."

"What do you mean you can't find Blaine?"

"We had a date tonight, and he never showed. When I last spoke with him, he was on his way but never showed. I can't get him to answer his phone. Do you know where he could be?"

Jessica became alarmed. With all that's happened, she dropped what she was doing and went to his place. His car was still in the driveway with the door open. She called the police. She wasn't sure what she would find. The police got there and searched the home, but Blaine was nowhere to be found. They searched for him in the area but to no avail..........

Blaine was awakened by a blast of cold water directly to the face. He tried getting up from the chair he was sitting in, but he noticed each ankle was secured to the legs of the chair. His hands were tied to the chair as well. He looked around for clues as to where he was. He looked up and saw a woman tied up as well. It was Erin. She was crying as she noticed the body of her partner-in-crime on the floor, fearing she would be next. Blaine saw the largely white male lying face up on the floor with blood coming from his head. He then looked at his captor.

"What do you plan on doing with us?"

"I plan on killing both of you. Blaine, you have been a thorn in my side ever since I moved here. I've been trying my best to make a family here, but you keep getting in the way. Do you think I didn't notice how you were cozying up to my fiancée? She acts as if she can't do anything unless *Blaine* says so. I couldn't permanently take her and the kids back to Baton Rouge because you have joint custody. No matter what I did, I could never rid myself of you, but all that's going to end today."

"So, it was you who killed all those women. Why?"

"For me, it was the thrill of the kill. But what better way to do it? I killed two birds with one stone. I got to enjoy hunting useless whores and then place the blame on you."

"You're forgetting your plan didn't work." Virgil looked stupid. He had nothing to say. He slapped Blaine in the mouth with the gun out of frustration.

"That plan may not have worked, but this one will. The both of you will die tonight. I'm going to stage the scene so it'll look like you died in a shootout with each other, and by the time they find your rotting corpses, I'll be long gone with my new family." Blaine looked at him in anger.

"So, this is your plan? You should know I won't let you get away with this." Blaine began threatening and taunting Virgil. He placed his gun in the back of his pants and stood over Blaine. He tightened the black leather gloves he was wearing and, with a balled fist, began hitting Blaine. 'When are you going to realize that this life is over for you? You no longer have a say in this matter." Virgil focused his attention on Erin. She had a look of fear and desperation. He could tell she was frightened. She didn't like the fact that Blaine was taunting him. He noticed her bulging eyes begging him to stop. He knew neither of them would make it out alive, but as a last-ditch effort to save Erin, he said,

"Why don't you let the girl go? It's me that you want."

"I can't do that. She's already been talking to the police. It's because of her that they made a break in the case. I've been watching the news. I heard they were dropping the charges against you because of her testimony, but Arthur will never talk." Virgil leaned over and looked at Arthur's face. He kicked his dead body.

"I've already taken care of him. He got careless when he brought this tramp along with him. They almost ruined my plans, but with both of you dead, I can take Sheila and my kids back to Baton Rouge and live the life we were meant to live." Blaine's cell phone began ringing. It was Jessica calling. Blaine had placed his phone's setting on silent mode earlier in the day while in a meeting with his attorney. He felt the vibration in his pocket. The loud buzzing of the device seemed to break the awkward silence in the room. He hoped that Virgil couldn't hear it.

Virgil stepped closer to Blaine, who was struggling to free himself from the ropes that bound him to the chair. He placed the gun to his head, "I'm going to love being a daddy to those boys. Oh, and don't worry, they'll get over you in due time, and my face will forever be etched in their memories. Because of the new life I'll give them, you'll become a distant memory."

"So, will you continue your career as a serial killer, or will you retire?" Blaine asked sarcastically.

"I don't know. If the mood hits me, I just may. I kill only when necessary."

"You won't get away with this."

"Yes, I will, I already have. I'm just tying up loose ends. Nobody knows I'm *"The Boss," Only the four of us; well,* three because Arthur won't tell."

Virgil had taken them to an old, abandoned warehouse on the corner of Maryland and Thayer Street off Twelfth Street in Little Rock. The area was very secluded. Nothing but abandoned boarded-up homes with hardly any traffic coming through. He could take his time killing them, and nobody would hear a sound. Blaine knew he had to survive somehow if only to keep this psychopath from his children. He watched as Virgil shot Erin twice in the chest. She screamed as the hot bullets tore through her body. The blast from the gun knocked her to the floor. He stood over her and shot her once more.

"Bitch! You should've kept your fucking mouth closed. I swear, I hate common street whores."

He kicked her in the side. He untied her and placed her by Arthur, staging her body. Virgil then turned his attention towards Blaine. Blaine looked at Erin, still writhing in pain on the floor, until eventually, she stopped moving.

"Man, you didn't have to shoot her. What's your issue with women? Why do you hate them so much that you can just kill them with such ease?" He looked at Blaine with a look of fury.

"You want to know why I hate them so much? Well, let me tell you why. My father was a great man who loved his family. He adored my mother. One of his clients invited him to a party. My father wasn't into parties but didn't want to lose this client's business, so, to appease him, he went. Well, someone brought a street whore. She knew what she was there for. She claimed my father and a few other men raped her. She testified against him in court, and he got a fifteen-year sentence, and we lost everything he worked hard for all those years. The family business he built from the ground up was ruined. Fifteen years in prison for one slut. My father was devastated. Prison life wasn't for him, so he killed himself. My mother struggled while raising me and my brother alone. I watched her work herself sick. When she died, my brother and I had to go to foster homes. They separated from us, and I haven't seen him since. The funny thing is, that bitch was on drugs and had abandoned her own kids. That was her choice. She destroyed her family and did the same to mine. When I got older, I found her ass. She was an old-ass drunk still trying to sell her pussy. I killed her with one hand, but before I killed her, I let her know who I was. While pleading for her life, she tried to apologize. Turns out she lied on my father. She got paid for the job that day, but she hid the money from her pimp. She said she accused my father of rape because her pimp was going to kill her for not coming up with the money. She lied to save her own ass. Yeah, that bitch deserved to die. As I felt the life seeping from her body, I experienced a high so exhilarating I had to do it again. I knew it was meant to be. Each time I feel the need for that high, I just think of all the whores who have destroyed families, and I go and eliminate one, and I feel better. I knew it was my mission to rid the earth of their measly existence, and that's what I intend to do. I'm a merchant of death. I was sent to do this. I will continue to exterminate them as long as I have breath in my body."

Out of curiosity, Blaine asked, "How many women have you killed so far?"

"I don't know, I've lost count, but imagine my surprise when I discovered you love whores. You coddle them by feeding and helping them, even bringing them into your home, and for what? So they can live to destroy another human being. You don't deserve those two boys. They don't need a father who has sympathy for whores. Sheila told me about how you were in the streets saving those bitches when you should've been home with your family. That's why your marriage failed. Now you think you're going to run my house from your house, telling me what I can and can't do with my family. For two years, I've put up with your shit. We couldn't plan a vacation without asking your permission. I'm sick of you interfering. I'm going to enjoy killing you. I'm going to kill you slowly. I'm not going to give you the satisfaction of dying a quick and easy death. I want you to suffer just as you've made me suffer."

He shot him in the foot. Blaine felt the heat going through as he heard his bone snap. Virgil untied him. He then shot him in the leg, yelling,

"Blaine, I tried to show you how it's done. That's why I had Arthur put you with that whore over in College Station. You were supposed to go down for that crime." He shot him in the side. Blaine began counting the bullets. He didn't know how many rounds it took for Virgil to kill Arthur; he counted three on Erin. He knew he had to be running out, but he didn't know if he had a second clip. he was sure he had enough to finish him off. "That little bitch that I stabbed in the car, I see you had to save her ass too. You're not fit to live just as they weren't. I'll see to it that you have a proper burial. I don't know why I didn't just kill you in the beginning. I wouldn't have had to go through all of this shit, but that would've made you a martyr, and I would've had to hear about you and how you were such a great man and father for the rest of my life. I needed your name to be disgraced so that the sound of it would cause your ex-wife and kids to cringe and never want it to cross their lips.

He shot Blaine in the abdomen, and with one more shot, he aimed at his chest. He didn't know where that shot landed, but it was actually in his shoulder. Blaine played dead. He could still hear Virgil breathing over him. He pulled him adjacent to Erin, then he staged the bodies with weapons, and he ran from the building. Blaine, who was barely breathing and trying not to black out, struggled to reach for his cell phone. He managed to call for help.

"911, what's the nature of your emergency." Breathing sporadically, he whispered,

"Need help, been shot." The operator on the phone asked,

"Sir, where are you?" He couldn't tell her. He lost consciousness. He was found after the police tracked him using the GPS signal on his phone. He regained consciousness in the hospital with Cindy and Jessica at his bedside. He tried to speak, but they told him not to say anything. His nose and mouth were covered with an oxygen mask. A tube had been placed in one of his nostrils to help him breathe better due to swelling. His mouth was swollen along with the complete left side of his face from being hit with the gun. He was frantically trying to talk, but he was so drugged on pain medicine that he couldn't speak. He only made muffling sounds. Thinking he would harm himself, the nurses were called in, and they pumped a little more pain medicine into him to calm him. He went back to sleep. In the meantime, Virgil caught a flight to Baton Rouge to be with Sheila. He was under the impression he'd killed everyone in the warehouse, but not only was Blaine alive, but Erin was also. She had yet to regain consciousness. Although she was clinging to life, her prognosis was good, and with much help, she was expected to make a full recovery. Armed officers were placed outside the doors of both Blaine and Erin. They wouldn't allow the news media to mention that they were still alive, and they went to the hospital under aliases.

Detective Armstrong was at the hospital as a friend and investigator into Arthur's death. They knew there was a connection because they found all three in the warehouse. They continued trying to piece the case together as they looked for the mysterious boss. Jessica called Sheila to tell her what happened with Blaine. Sheila was unaware that Virgil was behind the murders. She told him everything Jessica shared with her, and she insisted that they go back to Little Rock immediately to check on Blaine. Virgil was alarmed. He knew he needed to make it to the hospital to keep Blaine from talking. They caught a flight back to Arkansas. Virgil didn't know what he was going to do but he knew he couldn't just walk into the hospital with a gun and kill Blaine. He was trying to come up with a plan before he got there. He decided to just play it by ear. Virgil was exhausted, but he was desperate. He knew he had to keep Blaine from waking up.

After their plane landed at the Clinton National Airport, he got a rental car and proceeded to the hospital. He tried to stay calm, but his behavior became increasingly erratic. He was weaving in and out of traffic around the airport, almost hitting several cars. Sheila asked him to slow his speed. He entered the interstate at Bankhead Drive and got on I-440, heading west. He immediately hit the accelerator, his speed exceeding ninety miles an hour. He almost hit a few cars as he crossed over to the downtown exit. He entered Interstate six-thirty, finally getting off at the Pine and Cedar exit. He ran a few traffic lights. The children were afraid and so was Sheila.

"Virgil, you really need to slow down. You're going to hurt us or someone else on the road." Undaunted by her request, Virgil briefly looked at her but continued driving erratically. She looked back at her children. "Virgil babe, I'm going to have to ask you to slow down or let me and the children out of the car." By then they were coming to the back side of the hospital. They got parked, and they all went inside. Virgil began running, almost leaving them behind. They got the information they needed, and they had to be escorted by hospital staff. Nobody was allowed in to see Blaine without going through the screening process first. After being cleared by security, they were cleared and were allowed a visit.

Sheila and the children walked into the room. Seeing Blaine lying there was devastating to them. Blaine was heavily sedated and still unable to speak. His nurse was attending to his needs. Cindy and Jessica had left. The guard was outside the door. Sheila walked up to the bed. She was horrified when she saw his injuries. She placed her hand over her mouth. Her boys were crying out for their father. She reached out to touch his hand.

"Blaine, who could have done this to you?" she asked, sobbing. She wiped away a few tears. She comforted her boys. She lifted them one by one to kiss his cheek. Seeing her get that emotional about her ex-husband, Virgil was livid. He wasn't expecting that type of response from her. It angered him. It was all he could do to keep from killing Blaine on the spot. He pretended to care about Blaine and asked to be alone with him. He wanted to have a moment to reflect with him. Sheila reluctantly stepped out of the room. He walked over to Blaine's bed and whispered, "You're like a fucking cockroach. You refuse to die. I'm ending this shit right now."

He took Blaine's pillow from underneath his injured foot and took off his oxygen mask. He firmly pressed it into his face until Blaine began to turn blue. "Die already, damn-it," he said as he continued to press hard against his face. The machines were alerting the staff that he was in distress. By the time the nurse came in the room, Blaine was in peril. She saw Virgil smothering him with the pillow. He calmly walked out of the room and ran down the hall. He left Sheila standing there. The nurse was stuck between reviving Blaine and telling the guard. She chose to concentrate on Blaine. She pressed the alarm to alert the other staff members. Noticing all the commotion, Sheila called out to Virgil.

"Virgil, where are you going?" He didn't answer her. He continued to walk faster until he was down the hall. He sprinted on the elevator and out to the parking lot.

Sheila went into Blaine's room and the nurse yelled out, "Get the guard." Sheila did as she was instructed. The guard rushed into the room, and she told him what happened. By now, several hospital staff were rushing in. They went looking for Virgil, but he had already left the hospital. Sheila couldn't believe what she was hearing when the nurse told her that she caught Virgil smothering Blaine. She wondered why he would harm Blaine. It made no sense to her. She was immediately questioned by the police. She told the police what she knew, which was of no help. After they were convinced she had nothing to do with Virgil's plot to kill her ex-husband, she was allowed to go and comfort her children. Jessica heard what had happened and she rushed to the hospital. She comforted Sheila and the children. Blaine was moved to a different hospital. Since Virgil was still on the loose, Sheila and her children were immediately given police protection until he could be found. Little did they know, finding Virgil would prove to be next to impossible.

CHAPTER NINE

Eleven months later Virgil still hadn't been arrested. Many rewards leading to his arrest were offered. He'd been featured on national and local television programs. He had managed to elude the authorities. There were no signs of him. It was as if he had fallen off the face of the earth. During that time Blaine had gone through extensive therapy and had disciplined himself with a strict diet and a rigorous exercise regimen. He was almost back to normal. His foot gave him problems, but he was okay and was no longer walking with a cane. Cindy was still by his side, and their relationship was stronger than ever. Although Virgil never tried to contact Sheila, her and the children remained under police protection until he could be found. Jessica was back at work, and things were going well at the agency, but she felt uneasy that Virgil was still out there. She wanted so badly to see him punished for the pain he'd caused.

Blaine wanted to look for Virgil himself. Deep within, he had a score to settle, and he wanted to rough him up as he did with the child predator that cost him his job. Having his children in harm's way didn't sit well with him. He knew a man like Virgil deserved to die, and he secretly wanted to kill him. He planned on hunting him, forcing him to pay for his crimes.

Virgil settled in a small remote town off the Louisiana and Arkansas line near Eudora in Chicot County. He rented a small home in a secluded part of the area. Disguised as an elderly man, he would frequent neighboring towns to get some air sometimes even going over into Louisiana or Mississippi. The area was cozy; the locals were laid back, hardworking people, most of them not really paying much attention to current events. Nobody knew he was a killer. Not only was Virgil a killer, but he had been running drugs as a career and had a tiny stash of drugs and money. He lied and told Sheila he was running a legitimate business. His whole persona was based on a lie. He wasn't the man he pretended to be. He was checking out the scenery when he noticed a young Latina walking around. She was soliciting potential customers. She stood out from the locals in the area because there weren't too many of them in that area. She had on a short mini-skirt that was twisted sideways, and it looked a bit worn. Her black stilettos were leaning a little, and the back of them bore scuff marks. Her nail polish was worn with only traces left on her fingers. Her hair was tousled, not in any real style. It looked as though she had just gotten out of bed and barely dressed herself. He followed her for a few minutes with his eyes. After being turned down by many men, he called out to her. She made her way over to Virgil.

"What are you doing out here young lady?"

"I'm just trying to have a little fun, Papi; how about you? Are you looking for some fun?"

"What kind of fun are you looking for?"

"About two hundred dollars' worth." He got angry when she said two hundred dollars. He felt she was overselling herself, and given her appearance and the location, he didn't think she deserved that much. He was insulted because she didn't look at all presentable.

"Do you have a place you'd like to go and have this fun?"

"Why sure Papi." She said, excited, thinking she was about to make a little money.

They walked to his vehicle, and they both got in. He convinced her to go back to his place, only he didn't take her there. He went to another remote spot not far from there. He gave her the money. He wasn't worried because he knew he would get his money back. He had no intentions of allowing her to live long enough to spend it. She took the money and placed it in her bosom. She told him she had to use the bathroom. She stepped out of the vehicle, but it took her a while to come back. He quickly found her trying to skip out on him. He took her from behind and dragged her back to his vehicle. He then strangled her and dumped her body close by. The urge had come back. His anger towards prostitutes had increased. His need to kill had overtaken him. He went on the prowl looking for his next victim. He took the hunt methodically slow. He wanted to hand-pick his prey. He wanted to kill the next one slowly and enjoy the feel of it because his last kill was out of necessity and not pleasure. He couldn't find what he was looking for. He rode around all evening until he spotted a woman coming out of a beauty salon. He was quite charming, but she sensed something wasn't right with him. His mustache seemed to be a fake, which made him look odd. She quickly got in her car and left him there. A police car came down the street as she drove off. He held his head down as the officer's car came close to his. He let his window up and drove away. He looked in his rear-view mirror and watched as the police car made a U-turn in the middle of the intersection. He tried to pick up a little speed. The blue lights began flashing as the cruiser was fast approaching him. He decided to play it cool. His throat was dry, and his palms were sweaty. He gripped his steering wheel while quickly thinking of a story to tell the officer. He pulled over to the right of the road. The police car was blaring sirens along with flashing blue lights. He looked in his rear-view mirror. The officer's car was on his bumper. He then shifted to the left and drove past Virgil. Virgil's nerves were on edge. His heart was beating rapidly. He sat there for a few more seconds to gather his thoughts. He was spooked. He slowly drove off and decided to go back to his place for the night. Killing would have to resume another day, and so it did. Two days later. He found his prey.

Blaine was sitting in his living room doing some work for a client. He had the television on, but the volume was low, so he could concentrate on what he was doing. He glanced up at the screen and he noticed on the news a report of two female bodies being found. He turned the television up so he could hear. The way the bodies were found seemed random, but while hearing the story, Blaine had a feeling that he knew who the killer was. He looked up more on the story. He pinpointed the area where the bodies had been found on the map. He finished his work, and he went to the Barnes Detective Agency. Jessica was out, but her mother was there.

"Good evening Mrs. Barnes."

"Hi Blaine, how's it going?"

"I'm having a better day than yesterday; where's Jessie?"

"She went for dinner she should be back in about twenty minutes. At least I hope so because I'm hungry."

"Okay, well I'll be in my office. Tell her I want to see her when she gets here."

He began doing more research on his computer. He continued to look up crimes in the surrounding areas of the latest murders. Jessica finally made it back. She popped her head in and saw him looking at the computer.

"Hey Blaine, what's up? Mom said you wanted to see me."

"Yes, come around here for a second."

"What are you working on?" She looked at the computer screen. He had brought up towns near the murder sites.

"What's this all about?"

"Did you watch the news this morning?"

"No, I missed it, what happened?"

"There were two murders of women in these two towns, both near Eudora. The way the women were found, as described by the news, it looks very familiar. I'm willing to bet this is Virgil all over again. I bet he's right here in Arkansas. I mean, while everyone thinks he has fled the state or even the country he could very well still be here, but why?"

"When you are dealing with a psychopath there is no reasoning with them. If it's really him, something of great significance is keeping him here but what could that be? He's never tried to contact Sheila."

He looked at Jessica while she was still standing over his shoulder, looking at the computer, and asked, "Do you feel like going on a trip?"

"I'm ready when you are"

"That's my girl, you always have my back." They planned the trip. They didn't know how long they would be gone, so they packed for a two-week stay. Blaine was in it for the long haul. They rented a room and went canvassing the nearby towns. They rode around the areas where the bodies were found.

The locals thought it was a random killer and were hoping he had moved on, but Blaine had a hunch the killer was still there, and it was a matter of time before he struck again. He worked in one part of town while Jessica worked the other, sometimes meeting back up at their hotel and riding together. On a slow evening, they were sitting in a local diner. They noticed a grey 1990 Buick Sentry parking in front of the diner. A strange-looking man got out and went to a neighboring store. He looked old but he walked upright like a much younger person.

Jessica dropped her fork and said, "Hmm, will you look at that? What do you make of it? He walks kinda young to be as old as he looks. Look at his strut. I've never seen an old man with that much swagger." They both studied the man as he walked into the store. They got his license plate number. They decided to follow him. They fell back and followed him as he ran his errands. They ended up at a small home on an old dirt road hidden among the corn fields. They watched from a distance. Blaine watched him with his high-powered binoculars. He carefully studied the man.

"That's him, Jessica. Take a look." She grabbed the binoculars and watched as he entered his house and closed the door.

"Let's call the police and get them over here."

"No, let's watch him first and see what he's up to." They sat there for a couple of hours, but the man never resurfaced. Jessica stretched her legs.

"Blaine, I'm tired and I need to use the restroom. He's not going anywhere. Take me back to the hotel. We can come back later." Blaine reluctantly left. He dropped Jessica off and went back to the house. He was still home so Blaine watched and waited patiently. It was getting late. It was dark. He finally saw movement as Blaine predicted, Virgil waited to operate under the cloak of the night, a time when he knew desperate women worked the streets. Virgil got in the car. Blaine saw the headlights come on. He ducked as the car drove past him. He called Jessica and told her they were moving. She met up with him and they followed him together. He stopped at what looked like a small juke joint and went inside. They waited for about an hour until he came out. He had a woman on his arm. They got in the car and left. Blaine and Jessica followed as Virgil drove her back to his home. She called Blaine's cell phone

"What do you want to do Blaine?

"I'm not sure. Do you think the girl will be safe?"

"We have no way of knowing." While they were still on the phone, they saw the young woman running out of the house screaming at the top of her lungs. Virgil was in pursuit of her with a large knife chasing her as she ran down the secluded street. He had all but caught up to her when Blaine sprinted from his vehicle running towards them. Jessica was out of her car. Blaine caught Virgil and wrestled him to the ground while the young lady continued screaming. Jessica tried calming her to let her know she was safe.

She gave the girl her cell phone and yelled, "Call 911" The girl did as she was told, and Jessica went to help Blaine. Virgil wiggled himself loose from Blaine's grip and ran towards the back of the house near the fields of corn. Blaine and Jessica followed him, but it was pitch black so they couldn't see him. Virgil's eyes had adjusted to the darkness, and he watched as Blaine tip-toed past him. He leapt from the shadows with the knife still in his hand. He tried stabbing Blaine, but he moved out of the way just in time. Blaine grabbed him and they began to struggle. Hearing the commotion, Jessica followed the sound and was quickly upon them. Virgil was just about to plunge the knife into Blaine when she screamed, "Halt Virgil!" Virgil ignored her and kept after Blaine.

"I told you I would kill you and I'm going to keep that promise," he said to Blaine. Blaine knocked him to the ground with a karate kick to the jaw and they tussled for a few seconds. Jessica wanted to shoot but she couldn't see clearly, and she didn't want to shoot Blaine, so she watched them struggle. Blaine managed to wrestle the knife from him, and he buried it deep into Virgil's abdomen and twisted it. He withdrew it and plunged it back in again, this time leaving it inside.

Virgil looked at him and gave a sinister laugh. Still lying on the ground, Blaine scooted backwards and reached for his gun. He unsnapped the holster, got his gun, and put a round in the chamber. By then, Virgil had pulled the knife out of his stomach. Undaunted by his wounds, he ran towards Blaine again. Blaine emptied his gun into his chest. Jessica got off a few rounds herself that entered his body. She held the gun on him as Blaine made it to his feet. He kicked the knife away. He checked Virgil's pulse. He was dead. The sounds of sirens were heard in the distance. After the authorities began arriving, Blaine, Jessica, and the girl were questioned and taken to the local police station. Afterwards, they were released. Police and investigators searched Virgil's home, and they found multiple disguises, fake IDs, drugs and weapons, and rape kits. There was plenty of incriminating evidence from every crime scene and a diary praising himself for his many kills not only in Arkansas but all over the U.S. It took several months for the authorities to sort through everything. After a thorough investigation, they managed to solve many crimes from the nineties up to the present day. He kept photos and other mementos from his crimes. The story broke on the news that the killer was dead.

The Barnes Detective Agency received the rewards for solving the crimes. They were interviewed by the media. After a while, things began to die down. The news reporters went away, and life was getting back to normal for them. Jessica was gaining more cases from all the publicity. Although somewhat flattered, she and Blaine declined the many book deals and offers to make a movie based on their story, but she kept an open mind for the future. She was just glad her life was back to normal. Jessica's forty-third birthday was coming up. Blaine and Cindy hooked up with her mother, and her friend Marcus to throw her a surprise celebration at Cindy's place. Marcus was thrilled that Cindy and Blaine included him in the planning of the festivities. Marcus took Jessica to the club. She didn't suspect a thing. Cindy went all out for her birthday. She invited a few celebrity singers and other national performers to perform a show for Jessica's birthday. A select few of the state's local celebs and high-powered public officials were invited to the exclusive birthday party. Not only that, but Cindy also had her performers put on a wonderful show for Jessica. Her mother, Ms. Barnes, and Sheila were there, as well as Detective Armstrong, Lieutenant Fitz, and a few others from the LRPD. Jessica was moved by all the love and adoration she received. It was truly a great night and a wonderful birthday celebration. Jessica was able to let her hair down and relax with her friends. Although Jessica wouldn't express herself to anyone about her friendship with Marcus, it went without saying. Her loved ones knew how important he was to her, even without her admitting it to anyone.

She snuggled close to him not caring what anyone else thought. He took her by the hand and led her to the dance floor. It was apparent to everyone that he made her happy. After the night was over, Marcus took Jessica home. He was hoping she would invite him inside. He pulled into her driveway. He left the car running and walked over to the passenger's side to open her door.

"Aren't you going to come in?"

"Yes, I am," he said. He let out a sigh of relief. They went inside where they spent the rest of the evening enjoying each other's company.

Blaine and Cindy went to her home and spent a wonderful night together. All is well in their relationship until Cindy's past comes calling. *Follow that story in Arkansas Heat "Cindy's Revenge" Vol. 3*

Karen Coleman is an Arkansas native. She enjoys writing exciting and dramatic stories. A phenomenal author with a distinctive style, she has demonstrated a sensational talent for steering her readers through every line and page with eager anticipation.

Karen has published several novels in various genres. Readers have described her novels as riveting, fast-paced, and thrilling.
Her teen novels are insightful and empowering. As a mentor who has worked with teens for many years, Karen understands the social challenges they face, and she skillfully addresses those topics with a finesse that lends excitement, adventure, and encouragement.

A self-proclaimed writer of fiction with an element of truth, Karen began penning her thoughts as a hobby. After many years of writing and encouragement from those around her, she began writing on a more intense level, eventually turning out several wonderful novels. She offers something for almost every reader, from her adult crime series to her teen books, there's something to be enjoyed by all. Her literary works have garnered much fanfare and have not only been enjoyed by her many readers; she's highly celebrated among her writing peers. Her books are meant to inspire, uplift, and entertain, leaving her audience asking for more.

Karen is also a playwright, actor, and former city council member. She's the mother of four, and a Glam-ma of thirteen and counting. Her grandchildren affectionately call her Nana. She's also the proud mom of two rambunctious miniature schnauzers. When not writing or spoiling her grandbabies, she spends her time crafting, fishing, or enjoying a great barbecue.

OTHER BOOKS BY THE AUTHOR

Arkansas Heat "A City Scorned"

Arkansas Heat "A Brutha's Obsession"

Arkansas Heat "Cindy's Revenge"

Arkansas Heat "Deceptive Practice"

Arkansas Heat "Raising Delgado"

Closer Than Enemies 1

Closer Than Enemies 2

Frozen Dreams

In the Wrong Game

Metamorphosis "Good Girl Gone Bad"

Morgan's Path

No Place for Emily Ann

Whatever Happened to I Love You?

Also check out the audio versions on Amazon, Audible.com, and iTunes

www.ingramcontent.com/pod-product-compliance
Lightning Source LLC
Chambersburg PA
CBHW051252250626
47155CB00009B/3265